GHOSTLY VENDETTA

A PREQUEL NOVELLA TO THE CANDACE MARSHALL CHRONICLES

GHOSTLY VENDETTA

A PREQUEL NOVELLA TO THE CANDACE MARSHALL CHRONICLES

MICHELE ISRAEL HARPER

Love2ReadLove2Write Publishing, LLC
Indianapolis, Indiana

ALSO BY MICHELE ISRAEL HARPER

Wisdom & Folly Sisters: The Complete Story

The Candace Marshall Chronicles:

Ghostly Vendetta

Zombie Takeover

(Coming Soon)

Vampire Feud

Mummy Resurrection

The Beast Hunter Series:

Beast Hunter

Kill the Beast

Silence the Siren

(Coming Soon)

Quell the Nightingale

Slay the Wolf

Stop the Snow Queen

End the Fey

Coming Soon:

Altered Time Saga:

The Lady Bodyguard

The Lady Spy

The Lady Assassin

Standalones:

Queen of the Moon

Dreamworld

Tales of the Cousin Kingdoms:

Ruby Dragon Kingdom

Diamond Unicorn Kingdom

Sapphire Griffin Kingdom

Emerald Pegasus Kingdom

Time of the Dragons

To My Whole World:
My Savior.
Thank you for having such fun writing this with me.

CHAPTER ONE

"I'm not going."

Peter groaned. "Come on, Candace. It'll be fun. I promise."

I crossed my arms and shook my head. No way was he getting me to agree to that. Especially not that.

My boyfriend's mournful pleading morphed into annoyance. Directed at me. Again.

"I can't believe you're acting like this. It's just a party! A fun little party, no drinking, no sex, none of that other stuff you're so against."

"Yes, but—" My retort paused halfway out of my mouth. I cocked my head. "Wait. That *we're*—"

He cut me off, his words blending with mine.

"That *we're* so against. Right, right. Whatever. All I'm saying is, you're refusing to go for no reason. And I can't go without a date." His eyes took on a crafty glint. "Unless you want me to take Amber?"

I blinked. He wouldn't. The thought echoed around in my head like the pest it was. He saw my hesitation and went in for the kill.

"We'd be going as friends, of course, but I really see no other way around it. Not if you won't go with me. It's a couples' thing." He turned to leave, slinging his half-full messenger bag over his shoulder. "No problem. I'll just ask her."

My voice froze, mouth partway open.

He reached the doors of the library.

"Wait!"

His feet paused, right before exiting. I could practically hear the broad smile creeping across his face, he gloated so loudly. He looked back at me, face blank. Innocent. The gloating neatly tucked away.

"Maybe I could go for a little bit?"

I didn't know why I asked it like a question. Maybe part of me was hoping he'd release me from my stupid words. Without the whole asking another girl part.

I just didn't want to go. Why couldn't he respect that?

His steps beat a steady tread across the well-worn carpet, the smile on his face victorious. Mocking me. I was sure he didn't mean it that way, but that was how it felt.

He dropped a light kiss on my cheek, not bothering to check if the librarian was nearby to scold us. Or me, rather, when he'd conveniently disappeared.

"Thanks, babe. You won't regret it. I promise."

I watched him walk out of our college library.

Wouldn't regret it? I already did.

I hated Halloween.

Strobe lights pulsed. Music beats competed with each other over which one could burst eardrums first, and fog rolled through the giant house in waves from hidden fog machines.

Eerie shrieks and moans drifted around us. Coming close, fading away.

Did they have to sound so blasted real? I wanted to be anywhere but here.

I wrapped my red cape tighter around my body and wished it was one of those invisibility cloaks. I'd be outta here so fast.

Red lights near the ground bathed everything in the appearance of blood, and someone had added the occasional scream to the music mix. It. Was. Awesome.

As in, not at all.

Peter had disappeared the moment we'd entered the dwelling, leaving me standing alone, looking like an idiot.

Come to think of it, that wasn't much different than normal.

The hostess dropped a drink in my hand, not bothering to say hello. I sniffed the contents of the red cup.

I guessed what he meant by "no alcohol" was I didn't have to drink any. Cause it was present in abundance. This was *so* not my thing.

I moved out of the way of a stampede of guests and ran into a cobweb.

"Hey! Watch the decorations." The hostess, Cami, scowled at me.

She looked just as thrilled to have me here as I was to be here. She hadn't looked that way when she'd greeted Peter, just when she'd glimpsed me hiding behind him.

"Sorry," I mumbled as I tried to untangle myself.

Once free, though a few strands kept teasing me that I'd missed them, even though I swung my arms around and slapped my face and looked like an idiot, I aimlessly wandered about, searching for Peter, desperately trying not to notice the costumes.

I also may have been trying to put some distance between me and the hostess.

One kid looked like his neck was slashed, red dye spilling down his T-shirt. Another, fanged and vampired up. I hated vampires.

Witches, mummies, goblins, zombies in abundance — I wanted out.

I hated Halloween. I hated everything scary. I hated being here. And I'd overheard someone say the haunted house was next.

No. Freaking. Way. Not happening.

I tripped over a couple sitting in the most inconvenient spot possible and spilled my drink behind the couch. Cami—wherever she was now—was going to kill me. And no one would even know about it for days with all the fake blood.

You know what? Peter could just enjoy himself.

I turned to leave. Something big and hairy lunged at me, and I shrieked at the top of my lungs and fell back, right onto the floor.

A freaking werewolf.

Laughter wafted out from under the mask, and Peter ripped it from his head. No wonder he'd asked me to dress like Little Red Riding Hood.

"I got you so good! You should've seen your face." He bent over, hands on his knees, and howled with laughter.

My chest heaved, my heart pounded, and I desperately wanted to cry. Not the thing to do at parties. If ever.

"Peter! I can't believe you did that."

I tried to scramble off the floor, but my red cape kept twisting around my legs. I managed to get up on the third try, to the sound of a lovely, long *riiiiiiiiip*. Great, just great. The cape wasn't even mine.

And still no help from the werewolf.

He tried to look sorry. It didn't work. He shrugged. "You're so fun to scare."

My bottom lip trembled. I bit it into submission. "Can we go now? Please?"

He jerked the mask back over his head. Whoever had made that thing had way too much fun with it. Or they were intent on killing me with a heart attack.

My eyes wouldn't leave the rubber fangs, the grotesque snarl, the red eyes—Staring. At. Me.

Peter pulled me close and spun me into the living room. "Why, the party's just begun, my delectable treat. We can't possibly leave until I've gobbled you all up."

Zombies, witches, and one freakishly awful werewolf spun around me, over and over. I closed my eyes and tried not to open them again until we left.

Early the next morning.

CHAPTER TWO

"You want to do what?" I whisper-shrieked, trying not to disturb anyone in the college newspaper office.

Peter sighed and leaned back in his chair. "I'm hearing that an awful lot from you lately."

Never one to let my hands rest idly by while I was talking, I threw my free hand out and flung it around. "What? What have you been hearing from me?"

His sigh was deep and full of longsuffering. He waved a hand in my direction. "That. That whiney, scared, unadventurous thing you've got going on. Refusing to do something you know would be fun. Good for you, even."

My mind scrambled for what on earth he was talking about. The last time I recalled objecting to something he'd suggested was that awful party. Five months ago.

I glared at him. "That party was five months ago. And it was *not* fun."

He shrugged and looked back at his computer. "Yeah, taking you through that haunted house was just embarrassing."

I blinked. What? I had my eyes closed the entire time! I shook my head, hoping to clear it. Trying to focus on the bombshell he'd just dropped on me.

"You want to move? Just like that? The day after graduation?"

Peter tapped his pen against the desk and crossed his legs. Woman-style. I always thought he looked like such a sissy doing that. Other guys could nail it. Not him.

Of course, I'd never say such a thing to him. Not ever.

He leveled a condescending glare my way. "What are your plans after we graduate?"

"I—don't know—"

"Where are you going to move?"

"Um, well, I was thinking—"

"And what would that do to our relationship?"

"Uh . . ."

"Exactly."

He had me. Not only had I never dated anyone before Peter, I was convinced no one would want to date me if we ever broke up. A fact that had me clinging to him in a non-needy way. I swear. Can you say "Loser" with a capital "L"?

"Job prospects?" he continued.

He wasn't letting up, was he?

"Um . . ." I hadn't looked yet. I was too busy working every spare moment I had to pay my massive college bill. I'd managed it so far, but my final bill plus grad fees was on its way. Pretty sure it was more than I had, but I wasn't thinking about that right now.

Right now I had to deal with my life being planned for me.

I ducked my head and fiddled with the stack of papers I was supposed to be filing. Peter and I worked in the college's yearbook office. Also the school's magazine, newsletter, newspaper, and everything else writerly related.

If it needed to be edited, I did it.

And Peter pretty much ran it all. Or thought he did. When our boss wasn't there. And I did whatever he told me. To a degree.

"Nothing?" he prodded.

I stared at the papers before me, refusing to answer.

He breathed out a heavy sigh. "Candace, look at me."

My eyes lifted to meet his.

I didn't want to, but I did. Something just compelled me to do what people asked. Usually putting whatever I wanted on hold.

Like now.

He leaned forward, his manner intense. Urgent. "Think of how great this will be for m—us. Hired right out of college, in our chosen fields—"

It wasn't my chosen field, but I never bothered to tell him that, and he never bothered to ask. He just kept talking right over my inner turmoil.

"With great recommendations and even better pay."

I raised my eyebrow in spite of myself. "What's the pay?"

He squirmed, tugging at his tie. His smile was a little too bright. "A good question for the hiring editor."

"But . . . Acción? I've never even heard of it."

"It's a little town in New Mexico." He held up his hand at my first sign of protest. "Little, but highly recommended. It's a great place for experience. And a shoo-in for the *Albuquerque Tribune*."

Again, his dream, not mine. I crossed my arms, papers clutched to my chest, and raised an eyebrow.

"Come on." He rose and came toward me, placing his hands on my arms and rubbing them. Something he never did at work. Acknowledge me. Show any sign of affection. He said it got in the way. Of what, I didn't know.

My mouth parted, and I soaked in the attention.

"Start here, and you can go anywhere. I mean it. Besides, what will the distance mean for our relationship? What if you stay here? In Florida? Or even worse. What if you go home?"

A shudder passed through him. My eyes narrowed. Hey, I was the only one allowed to hate my small town in the foothills of California. Not that he'd ever been.

For pretending to hate Jasper so much, he certainly was eager to move to Acción, another small town. Besides, even though I wanted nothing to do with where I'd grown up, I didn't appreciate his tone. It was my home, after all. Warts and all.

It was just a saying. Promise.

He lowered his voice and tried that puppy-dog look on me. At work? He must be desperate.

"I care about you. About us. I don't want to lose you, Candace."

I squirmed and glanced around. No one was paying attention to us. Probably cause most people who'd known Peter for awhile avoided him like the plague. Something I hadn't quite figured out why yet.

But I needed that money. And I didn't want to go home after school. And I had no job interviews lined up. None. I would at least know Peter there . . .

I sighed. "Fine. Yes, I'll go."

Peter whooped and wrapped me in his arms. "You won't regret it."

I started to melt into him, but he pulled away before I had a chance to. He plopped in his chair and spun away, dialing rapidly.

"Fred? Yes, hello. She said she'd do it. Excellent. May I send her your contact info?"

I tried to hand him the folder I'd first come over to give him. He waved me away and turned his back even more.

"You'll contact her? Perfect. Here's her cell."

My mouth dropped open.

He rattled off the numbers, not even asking me if he could do so, nor even bothering to tell me who this Fred person was and why on earth he'd be calling.

"Yes, we'll be there. Together. We graduate next month, so we'll see you then. You already have our résumés and portfolios that I sent you? Perfect. Thank you. Bye."

He slammed the landline down and pounded away at his keyboard. I tried to hand him the file again, but he jerked away, clearly annoyed.

"Some other time, okay? I'm kinda busy."

I slammed the file onto his desk, spilling the contents and half the junk on his desk onto the floor.

"Hey!"

I turned and marched away, shoving the rest of the files onto a filing cart as I passed. If my entire life was being planned for me—including high school, first job, college, and now my career path, then I was going to do the one thing I actually enjoyed.

Before someone took that away from me, too.

CHAPTER THREE

I lined up the shot, adjusted the lens, the aperture, and the ISO settings. Squeezing the shutter button gently, I waited until I had the perfect shot.

There.

The shutter clicked in rapid succession.

I pulled the DSLR camera away from my eye and quickly scrolled through the pictures I'd just captured.

Perfect. Beyond perfect.

Resting my elbows on the pier's railing, I cradled my dream in my hands and breathed a deep, contented sigh.

Sunsets were breathtaking in Florida, but the dolphins I'd just captured with the sun's final rays glancing off them? Most likely my best work.

And no one would ever see it.

Because my parents and boyfriend agreed. Photography wasn't a real job.

My phone buzzed. I pulled it out of my pocket and glanced at the lit screen.

How 'bout some pre-wedding shots?

A slight grin touched my face. My fingers tapped on the screen.

You mean more?

What? A girl can never have too many pictures. Especially of her smoking-hot man.

I laughed out loud. Jemma told everyone just how handsome the man she was going to marry was. All the time.

Sure. What time?

Jemma quickly replied with the where, when, and whatever. Her words, not mine. I grinned and saved it to my phone.

It's on my calendar. See you tomorrow.

Awesome! Thanks! You bringing that good-looking man of yours? Any hint of when you'll tie the knot?

The sarcasm was strong with that one.

The thought soured in my stomach. Probably not the best reaction to the M-word. I hesitated. I knew Jemma tried to like Peter for my sake, and she'd long ago stopped telling me to date a few other guys. Just to see. But I could tell she still wanted to.

I debated my response, but all I came up with was, *Not yet.*

Uh-huh. Tell him not to wait too long, or he'll lose you to someone way better. You can quote me if you want.

I shook my head, my grin slowly making its way back to my face.

Jemma might be living her dream with Mr. Right, but mine didn't look like they were coming true in any shape or form. And marriage definitely wasn't one of them. The thought made me want to run for the hills. If there were any in Florida.

Pretty sure there weren't.

I tapped out a quick reply. *Whatev. See you tomorrow.*

See ya, Chica.

I dropped my phone back into my camera bag and gathered my equipment in the deepening dusk. I needed to learn just a tad more before I could take night shots.

CHAPTER FOUR

Footsteps stomped toward me.

"That was childish, you know," Peter accused.

I didn't look up from my book. "It was."

"I had to organize everything."

I wasn't in the mood to play nice. "How sad for you." I flipped a page.

Peter sprawled a hand across my textbook. "And very unprofessional of you."

My eyes lifted. I glared. He looked uncertain for the first time since I'd met him four years ago at a freshman welcoming party. One I was hosting, because I'd already been here for two years.

Hey, I worked my butt off to pay for college myself with no loans. And that meant taking fewer classes than most and working more jobs than most.

Though I'd be the first to admit changing my major three times hadn't helped.

A frown flitted across his face. "Do you not want to go to Acción?"

I sighed and leaned back, stretching my neck before answering him. "I don't know. I don't *not* want to go to Acción, if that makes sense. I just would've appreciated being asked first. Being a part of the decision. Of the planning."

"Oh. Is that all."

I glared at him. "Yes. That's all."

"Your parents think it's a good idea. Your brother too."

My brother was in on this? Since when? I was going to kill him.

My eyebrows shot up. "And you never thought to ask me if *I* thought it was a good idea?"

Peter sighed. "Maybe you're studying too hard, Candace. You haven't been acting like yourself lately. Do you want to talk about this after graduation?"

My glare hadn't slipped. "Would that be before or after our flight to Acción?"

He swallowed. "During?"

"Ugh!" I swatted his hand away and stared at my textbook, hoping nothing on the page that blurred before my eyes was on my final.

He couldn't ask what I wanted? Just once? I stilled.

Would I even be brave enough to tell him?

"Okay. Well, when you're ready to talk, find me." He turned and stalked away.

I watched him go. Unwanted, ridiculous tears sprang to my eyes. I was not letting those suckers fall.

They kinda had a mind of their own and did so anyway. Traitors.

Peter wanted me to move away from everything I knew, everything I hoped would happen after graduation, just to follow his dream? Did he really think I'd be happy?

I stared unseeing at my textbook. And that meant I'd have to talk to Jemma . . .

Oh my gosh, she was going to kill me.

I groaned and dropped my head into my hands. Could I please stand up for myself? Just once?

"What?" Jemma bellowed.

Bridezilla had nothing on the heaving ball of fury before me.

"I'm sorry?" I asked.

"You gave your word, Candace. Does that mean nothing to you?"

I rubbed my eyes, burning with fatigue and unshed tears. "I know. I told him I'd go . . ."

"Not to him. To me." Jemma pointed off to her side, then to herself, punctuating each word.

I cringed and covered my eyes with my hand. I had no excuses. None.

"My boyfriend told me to" wouldn't cut it with Jemma. It shouldn't cut it with me, either, but I was so stinkin' exhausted from trying to make everyone else happy. I didn't know what to do. The right thing to do.

I sighed. "I know. But he said the job wouldn't still be there if we didn't leave right away."

"That no good, lying, son of a—" She stopped herself and placed her hands on her hips. "And a job you don't even want is more important than your best friend?"

My head jerked up. My hand fell away from my eyes, and I stared at her with my mouth open. She considered me her best friend?

"What am I going to do now, Candace? I hired you to photograph my wedding. *My wedding.* The week after graduation. What am I going to do—hire Greg?"

I slammed my eyes closed. "Please don't do that. Please."

"Why?" Jemma demanded.

Because he's awful. Because he thinks a blurry picture isn't a problem. Because he misses big moments and captures unimportant ones.

Like a freaking red plastic cup when something far more

important was going on in the background. Like a high school grad party. I wasn't bitter. Not at all.

"Just . . . don't."

"Look at me, Candace."

I peeked at her, not wanting to at all. Why was everyone telling me to look at them? I'd rather retreat behind my eyelids when things got scary.

"You won't even say it?" Sadness tinged her voice.

I cocked my head. "Say what?"

"That you're one of the best photographers I've ever seen, and Greg can't take pictures worth spit compared to you?"

My eyes widened. She thought that? About me?

Jemma huffed and rolled her eyes. "Yes, Candace, you're the best. Even if I could pay someone else less, I'd still hire you. You amaze me." Her eyes filled with tears. "And I want you to capture my wedding into forever. No one looks at things the way you do."

The tears did it. I had to explain to Peter why I'd be missing our flight.

I'd rather face the haunted house again.

CHAPTER FIVE

"You *what*?" Peter screeched.

I shied away, fiddling with a plant nearby. Yes, a plant. I have no idea why. It was there, and my hands needed to be busy.

I just hoped the stupid thing wasn't poisonous.

"I gave my word, Peter. I have to do this."

"Do what exactly?"

The plant's leaves got real interesting. Fast. I scrutinized the life out of those suckers.

"Oh, you know. Stuff. So I'll still be there. Just . . . later."

Peter closed his eyes and dropped his head back. It looked crazy uncomfortable.

"Let me get this straight. You told me you'd come with me, then all of a sudden, you remembered you'd conveniently 'promised' someone else"—he did air quotes, his head still back at that awful angle—"something, and that trumps any promise you made me?"

I scrunched my nose. "Kind of?"

He dropped his head forward, shaking it and muttering under his breath.

"I have to do this, Peter. I have to. I'm sorry. Why is this so important to you, anyway? I can always come later."

He raised incredulous eyes to meet mine. "Are you serious?"

"Yeah. Can't you just go there without me? I can always—"

"I just can't, okay?"

"But why? You don't need me there at first. Just go, check out apartments, get to know the town a little, start working without me, just for a little while—"

"I said I can't."

I threw my hands out to the side. "But why? That's ridiculous! Why don't you just—"

"Because they won't hire me without you!" he snapped.

My mouth fell open.

What? No wait. What?

It seemed to be the only thing my brain was capable of thinking. Yet nothing made its way to my tongue.

Another student walked by, drawn to our loud voices and very public argument.

I'd chosen a busy place on purpose, hoping it would make it easier to tell him without him killing me on the spot, but now the stares were making me uncomfortable. Like, crazy uncomfortable.

I was pretty sure all five thousand students on our campus had decided to walk by this very spot at this very moment and stare Right. At. Me.

I was so done being the center of attention.

He stepped close and dropped his voice. "I should've told you earlier, okay? I'm sorry I didn't."

"B-but, I thought they only needed me for a copy editor? The same thing I do here. Well, one of the things . . . Isn't a reporter more important?"

"They do. It is." He sighed. "Apparently they need an editor badly enough, if you don't come, they aren't going to hire me either."

He flushed. I think it was the first time in his life he'd been told someone else was more important than he was.

And that someone was me.

A smile blossomed on my face. They really, truly, actually wanted me? *Me?*

"Don't ruin this for me, Candace."

My head jerked up at the low growl, and the smile died on my face. He inched closer, dropping his voice even further.

"I mean it. I've got to have this job. I already told our boss we'd both be there the day after graduation."

I cocked my head, my brow furrowing. "I thought you said you could get any job at any paper?"

"I can. But I want this one."

"Why?"

"Because I do, okay? You wouldn't understand."

I stared at him, wanting to ask more, to find out why this was so important to him. But Peter didn't like to be questioned, and he definitely didn't want to continue this conversation. I could tell.

I nodded. "Okay."

He blinked. "That's it? Okay?"

"Yeah. I'll explain everything to him. Then he'll still hire both of us, and I can start a little later than you. No problem."

Peter opened his mouth, but this time I cut him off.

"I should probably call him now so he has time to plan. Fred, right? See ya."

I darted away.

Peter called after me. "What are you going to say?"

I waved and sprinted toward the girls' dorm. Once inside, I slowed and let my excitement add a bounce to my step.

Maybe they'd seen my pictures. Maybe they'd move me to something else quickly. Like photography. Maybe they'd seen the thousands of things I'd edited and really did think I was good at it.

I stepped into the elevator and punched the key to the seventh floor.

I had no idea. But it had to be good. My smile couldn't be stopped.

Maybe I wanted this job after all.

CHAPTER SIX

"Perfect. Thank you, sir. See you then."

I hung up the phone, my insides doing the happy dance I desperately wanted to let out.

Mr. Fred MacGyvver—the coolness of his name wasn't lost on me—my new boss, was professional, kind, courteous, and treated me like an adult. I instantly liked the man.

Maybe Peter would learn a thing or two when we moved to this new town.

"Acción . . ." I rolled the town's name over my tongue, enjoying the feel of it. *Action* in Spanish.

I scooted my chair closer to my desk and pulled up info about the town on my laptop.

Acción boasted a dome theater, one major factory, a few museums, and lots of mom and pop shops on its main street. The population wasn't much, but it looked like a boost to its economy was attracting new families.

Hence the attractive job openings at a rapidly growing paper.

It was roughly two hundred miles from Albuquerque, where Peter wanted to work next, and the info on the town's website was hip, cool, and looked like it could be a fun and safe place to raise a family.

Not my immediate life goals, let me tell you.

Besides, all of that did nothing to camouflage how small the town really was.

My heart sank a little. The specs weren't all that different from my hometown, Jasper, California. Jasper was set in the foothills, not incredibly far from San Francisco. If I wanted to explore the big city, which I did frequently, or the Sierra Nevadas for a hike, Jasper was a good little town. A beautiful town.

But I'd always felt trapped there.

My dream was to live in a big city, surrounded by millions of bustling people. Constant action. Getting lost in the crowd and not having every action scrutinized. Gossiped over. Pulled apart for inspection.

Like maybe New York.

I shook my head, my thoughts getting too deep and desperate for even me. Every time I thought of my future, it felt like a hand clutched my throat and squeezed.

I hated that feeling.

Pulling my schedule from its folder, I scrunched my nose and studied it. Only a million, bazillion things to do for graduation, not including finals.

Ugh. Finals.

My heart sank as my eyes found the final, bolded, italicized, and underlined—seriously, had someone gone formatting happy?—sentence at the bottom of the page.

Diplomas and final grades will not be released until your school bill is paid in full.

All the air felt like it'd been sucked out of the room. I'd been working so hard. Taking any extra job I could get while still maintaining my grades. I worked my butt off for those A's and the occasional B.

And I was determined to graduate debt-free and not take

out a loan for any part of my tuition. Which is why I'd worked for a full year after high school and saved enough to pay for my entire first year of college.

It was the next four years after that that had been killer.

I didn't want to know what my final bill was. I really didn't.

With shaking hands, I slit open the envelope and pulled out my final bill, due the month before graduation.

My mouth fell open. There were so many numbers. I didn't have that.

I read it again.

$5,897.53.

Oh, is that all? That couldn't be right.

I dug out my checkbook, bank statements, and college bill statements for the semester and frantically went through them all. I was positive I didn't owe that much.

Numbers fell into place, and I did in fact owe exactly that.

I pounded my head on the desk and instantly regretted it. "Ow!"

Why was that a thing? I needed my brain and skull intact in order to find a way to pay this bill and freaking graduate already.

I crumpled the bill, threw it in the wastebasket—made me feel just a little better—then retrieved it and smoothed out all the wrinkles. $5,897.53. Yep, still there.

I knew it was going to be a lot, but yikes.

I mean, I was grateful the school had worked with me, letting me work on campus for summer and Christmas breaks while taking a class or two, but still. That was a *lot.*

I stuck my bill in my folder, slung my messenger bag over my shoulder, and headed out the door. Not that I hadn't been doing so already, but time to do everything in my power to make the loan I clearly was going to have to take out as little as possible.

Stupid, freaking loans. I hated being in debt.

CHAPTER SEVEN

"Thank you so much! That's perfect!"

I beamed as yet another senior signed his name with an illegible scrawl on my sign-up sheet.

Apparently Jemma wasn't kidding when she said she bragged about my photographs all the time.

I flipped through the stack of papers in my hands. Set around my campus job, my two off-campus jobs, my classes, and my finals, my schedule for senior pictures, day-of-graduation pictures, and group shots was full to bursting.

How awesome was that?

I squealed and did a ridiculous little jig, right there in front of God and every person at my school.

"Hey, are you that chick who's taking senior portraits?"

My face filled with heat, and I couldn't think of a blasted thing to say. "Uh . . ."

"Well? Yes or no?" The brunette beauty propped her hand on one hip and tapped a toe. She hadn't talked to me in four years. She was way too cool to even acknowledge my existence. Until now.

I gulped. "Yeah, sure, that's me."

She eyed me up and down. "I've seen your stuff. Nice work."

I tried to speak around the shock about to knock me unconscious. "Uh . . . th-thanks. Thanks . . . you. I mean, thank y—"

She rolled her eyes and spoke over my stupidity. "So tell me why I should hire you when my picture's already been taken for the school yearbook?"

Because those pictures are stuffy and crazy posed, with more plastic smiles than should be legal.

But of course I didn't say that out loud.

Instead, I wordlessly handed her my portfolio, already open to one of the yearbook staff's portraits.

Although she tried to keep her bored, unaffected-by-anything look on her face, her eyebrows climbed her forehead. "Not bad." She swiftly flipped through the rest of the portfolio, then started at the beginning. "Really good, in fact." She slapped it closed and handed it back. "Sign me up."

I fumbled for it and ended up dropping everything else I had in my arms—except for my clipboard. I cringed. Face a million degrees hot, I ignored the pile at my feet and flipped to the final two slots I had available.

"Th-this is what I have l-left, here and here. Payment is due up front, and if you miss your session, no refunds."

Her eyes flitted to the price I'd listed, and she didn't even bat an eye. "Deal." She signed her name with lots of squiggles and hearts—in both time slots.

My jaw may have dropped onto the pile at my feet.

She dug in her satchel and pulled out a checkbook. She flipped me around and wrote on my back, and all I could do was hold perfectly still and try not to breathe—while staring at the mess at my feet. Ugh.

"Here."

I slowly turned and accepted the check thrust out to me.

"See you then!"

With a snap to her gum, she walked past me, skirting the mess I'd made.

I stared at the check in my hands, also covered in squiggles and hearts. And squealed. Like a little girl. And did another crazy jig.

Because I wanted to be known as *that* girl. The crazy one.

I checked my watch. Yep, I still had a watch. I was that awesome.

Just enough time to deposit all the checks in the on-campus bank, then head to my next class. I'd made over a grand merely signing every free moment of my life away to every other person on campus.

Which meant I was that much closer to paying my bill without a loan.

"Yes!" I squealed. Again.

I spun around to attack the spilled books, papers, and other nonsense I'd dropped everywhere, but it wasn't there. Nope. Jackson was holding it all in a neat stack.

The Jackson.

I froze.

A girl in my dorm had the biggest crush on him and would spiral into depression for weeks if he smiled in her general direction. We all hated to even think about the time he'd said her name with a "hello" attached to it.

I think the entire floor secretly plotted to have her moved to another dorm building.

At another school.

All this flashed through my mind, as he stood there, smiling at me. At *me*.

Oh, please just hand me the books and walk away.

He did no such thing.

"I believe these are yours?"

He smiled at me, and I may have sighed. Aloud. I snapped upright and grabbed the books and papers out of his hands.

And his hands brushed mine.

My heart lurched crazily in my chest, sweat popped out on every inch of my body, and I jerked away with a gasp.

What, was I like, twelve? I mean, seriously.

He grabbed the strap of his messenger bag and settled in, as if he intended to have a conversation with me.

Oh please no. I'm not any good at that!

"Candace, right?"

I gulped and bobbed my head with that freakishly annoying bobblehead thing I've got going on sometimes.

"You work at the market across the street, right?"

I nodded.

"And the drugstore on weekends?"

I nodded again.

"And the school newspaper?"

I froze mid-nod. Oh my gosh, was he some creepy stalker, hiding behind incredibly good looks and blazing white teeth? That secretly smitten part of me didn't seem to care.

Next they'd be asking *me* to move out of the dorms.

"I saw you at the beach this weekend."

"Oh, uh, yeah." I let out a strangled giggle, then cringed. *Why, Candace, why?*

I'd seen him too, and I'd promptly run away. Jemma had stayed and chatted, but no matter how much she'd waved me down, I'd pretended not to notice and had gotten as far away from the hot-guy club as I possibly could.

A gangly klutz like me had no business even looking at what I couldn't have.

"You ran away."

"Oh, did I?"

Not only did my voice sound vapid, an airy, not-at-all-like-me laugh escaped my mouth, and I wanted to die. Literally. Right now. Die.

He chuckled. "You did."

"So, uh . . ." I thrust out my hand. "Nice seeing you again."

Wrong move. He took my hand in his in a single shake, and

my palms immediately went clammy. Plus he was touching me, so my brain fritzed out.

Way to betray me, body.

I pulled my hand away, every fiber of my being on fire, and turned to run away.

"Bye!" I called over my shoulder.

Of course, being me, I slammed into someone. Papers flew everywhere. Again. But this time, I didn't bother to pick them up. I kept running.

Clipboard and checks clutched to my chest, heart in my throat, humiliation off the charts—I was never going to be able to show my face outside my dorm again.

CHAPTER EIGHT

Peeking around the edge of the building, my breath left me in a whoosh, and I sagged against the wall.

No Jackson. Thank God.

I never wanted to see him again, not for the rest of my life. Not after the way I'd acted.

Would there ever come a time when I didn't act like an idiot? I hoped so. Desperately. But for now, I simply had to evade Jackson at all costs.

At least I still held the clipboard and checks in my hands when I'd come out of my haze, standing in my dorm room, gasping for air. Pretty sure I'd run all seven flights of stairs, but it was all a little hazy.

But it would explain the whole not being able to breathe thing.

I'd have to deposit them later.

After another quick check, I slipped around the corner and headed to class. Now I needed to somehow get my schedule, my finals notes, and every other important thing I'd flung at some stranger back ASAP. Including my final bill.

But no way was I asking Jackson.

I groaned. How could I have been so stupid?

Peter strolled by, chatting with a buddy of his, and gave me a stony nod.

Just as he was about to pass me without saying a word, I gasped and jumped in front of him, clutching his shirt. "You can do it!"

He gave me an annoyed look, not missing a beat of his conversation.

"I'm sorry, excuse me? Sorry to interrupt, but—" I dug around in my bag. "Can you do me a huge favor?"

Peter and his friend did the manly clasp-hands-then-hug thing. "Hey, man. Catch you later."

Peter's friend gave him a quick wave and me a quick smile and walked off.

Peter looked over my head at the clock tower. "You're going to be late."

"I know! I know." I still dug around in my bag.

You'd think with so many missing papers, these checks would be easier to find.

"Aha!" I came up with them and waved them in his face. "Can you please deposit these for me?"

I said it all rushed and desperate, not knowing the next time I'd be able to slip away to the on-campus bank. Or wait in the lines that stretched to infinity and moved like molasses in winter.

He flipped through them, looking impressed. "Whoa. Where'd you get this much money?"

I plucked them out of his hands and swiftly scribbled what could hardly be considered my signature all over the backs. "It's called hard work."

No way was I telling him I was doing something frivolous like photography.

I finished, stuffed them in an envelope, and jotted my account info on the front. I held them out to Peter. "Please. I know you have a free period right now."

At first, he looked annoyed, then a look came over his face

I couldn't decipher. He grinned and took the envelope from me. "I would be happy to."

"Oh, thank you!" I gave him a quick hug, which he didn't return, and ran for the closest building. "I really appreciate it!" I called over my shoulder.

"Hey, what did Mr. MacGyvver say?" he yelled after me.

"Tell ya later!" I called back as I darted into the building. Pretty sure he didn't catch any of that.

I took the elevator with a gaggle of students and made it to my fifth-floor Calculus class in plenty of time. As I walked, I closed my eyes and took a deep breath.

Made it. And my checks were safely on their way to my account. Score!

And now my favorite class of the day.

I loved math. I loved everything about school, for that matter! It made me feel so smart, putting everything down on paper and figuring things out in an orderly fashion, just me, myself, and my paper.

Homework just made my day better.

My inner critique ran with that one, but I shushed it. *I'm the weird one, remember? Deal with it.*

My eyes popped open seconds later, and I smiled as I beelined for my classroom.

And stopped. My smile died a quick death. Some student plowed into me from behind.

"Hey, watch it!"

It was enough to get Jackson's attention.

That devastatingly handsome smile was back on his face, and he headed straight for me, leaving the girl he'd been talking to with the perfect sightline to glare daggers at me. Whoever she was.

You can have him! I wanted to shout. *I wouldn't know what to do with him anyway!*

Plus, I didn't want Queen of a Broken Heart in my dorms to come after me. That girl was scary.

Plus, boyfriend. I blinked. Oh my gosh, Peter! I hadn't thought of him once since Mister Gorgeous had derailed my brain. Um, oops?

Jackson stopped in front of me and pulled out a stack of papers in one smooth motion, making it look like art.

Of course. Because why not? God couldn't have spread around the suaveness and the graciousness and the gorgeousness. Oh, no. He had to give it all to one person. Jackson.

He held out the papers. "I believe you dropped these. Again."

I just stood there, eyes wide, lips parted, brain screaming, *Danger, danger, danger!*

Not again. Oh, please, not again.

He shifted them toward me just a little more. My eyes darted toward the redheaded girl still glaring our way, and her gaze got even more hostile, if that were possible.

With a gentle smile, he pulled my bag off my shoulder, flipped it open, and slid the papers neatly into an open spot. My eyes followed his every move.

His stack was the only non-messy thing about my bag. Figures.

Without asking my permission, he slid the bag back over my shoulder, and his fingers danced along my skin.

I gasped, and every head whipped our way.

I closed my eyes and moaned. Why oh why had I worn a sleeveless shirt today? Why oh why did my every thought end up on my face? Why oh why did I have to react in front of the entire school?

Jackson cleared his throat, and I peeked at him. His grin was far too delicious to be directed my way. *Stop already. Just stop.* He didn't.

"Walk you to class?"

Why, yes, because I can't manage that three feet by myself. I might get mugged. Or trip. Or die from embarrassment.

Actually, all three real possibilities in my case.

I glanced at the girl, who had shifted forward slightly, looking like she was ready to pounce.

Or Miss Perfect over there might just do me in herself.

"I have a boyfriend," I blurted.

His smile tightened, and he glanced around as my loud voice ricocheted down the hall to a few answering snickers.

"Yes, I know." He looked just about as pleased as Jemma did when I brought up Peter. "I was actually wondering if you had any slots left for senior pictures."

I blinked. "Oh. Um . . ."

Please somebody just shoot me now. He wasn't interested in me—which I freaking knew already—he was just being a nice guy and wanted pictures. Oh. My. Gosh.

Thank God my schedule was full.

I gave one fast, furious shake of my head. "Full up, sorry."

"Well . . ." He shoved his hands in his pockets and looked down, rocking up on his toes and back down. "If a spot opens up, will you let me know?"

He shoved a paper in my direction, and I took it out of reflex. I glanced down. His number. Claxon sirens drowned out every rational thought. He freaking gave me his *number*!

For business. For business only. Nothing more.

"Oh. Um. Yeah. Sure. Why not?"

The bell rang, and I jumped a mile.

He smiled again as he looked at me. "Don't be late."

"Oh, okay. I won't." But I already was.

Neither of us moved.

"Call me if you have an opening."

I opened my mouth to say, *I will,* but I couldn't, because that would be lying. "Uh . . ."

He jerked his head to the door behind him, his smile something delicious to behold. "Go on."

I glanced past him. Apparently glaring girl was up for late demerits too. What *college* still had a demerit system? I mean, really.

Her glare did for me what I couldn't do for myself. I moved to walk past him. He grabbed my arm. I jerked away and stared at him with wide eyes.

He shoved his hands in his pockets again and looked as though he felt a smidgeon of the embarrassment I felt on a daily basis.

"Hey, um, I wanted to tell you about something?"

I raised an eyebrow and tried to pretend I hadn't wrenched my arm away as though I didn't want him touching me. Cause my traitorous feelings were precisely the opposite of that, and I was pretty sure that would horrify him just as much as it did me.

Boyfriend. Right.

"There's this contest. Well, a dare, really. Well, it's sponsored or something. I don't really know."

My eyebrow climbed higher. Smooth Jackson, at a loss for words?

"The prize money's five grand." He shrugged, not quite meeting my gaze. "I just thought, you know, maybe you could enter that if you, you know, needed the money or something."

I gasped. "You looked at my school bill?"

Glaring girl huffed and stomped to class, apparently giving up. I didn't spare her a lick of my attention. Things started getting hazy for an entirely different reason.

"I didn't. Honest. It fell out of your folder, and I put it back. I didn't mean to see it."

Anger flushed through me, hot and fast, and I jerked my bag away from him, as though it dangling next to his body would somehow contaminate it.

"I don't need your help, I don't need you going through my stuff, and I most certainly won't be calling you if every person on campus decides to cancel!"

His eyes widened. "Candace, it's not like that, I promise —"

I huffed and stomped away, all rational thought fleeing. Scratch that. It was long gone, for a while now.

Most kids had loans or wealthy parents to cover their bills, but oh no. Not me.

I had to be the one person on campus who absolutely freaked out about debt—losing a house and most of your stuff as a kid would do that to a person—and I refused to get any kind of loan. My parents told me if I wanted to go to college, I'd have to pay for it myself. So I had. Till now.

I didn't even have a credit card.

And no credit meant no credit history which made taking out a loan nearly impossible. Leaving me with no idea how I would even freaking graduate.

And sending my emotions on an endless rollercoaster.

My feet carried me into class as an angry swarm of thoughts buzzed around my head. Now I was certainly never going to look at or speak to Jackson again. I didn't even care that I wasn't being rational. My pride had been wounded.

Not that I had an awful lot of that to wound, but still.

The classroom was completely quiet, and Mr. Matthews met my gaze with that tiny smile of his that made students everywhere think he had a secret life. There may or may not have been bets going on of what he truly did for a living.

Mine were on secret agent, trailing someone at this very school.

"So glad you decided to join us, Miss Marshall. Won't you please have a seat?"

I stomped to my seat on the front row and slammed my bag next to my desk, fuming the whole way. How dare he?

"Now that we're done getting a peek into Miss Marshall's personal life, shall we go over what will be on the final?"

I groaned and dropped my head in my hands as several uneasy chuckles slid through the room.

How dare he.

And this time, I wasn't sure which "he" I was talking about.

CHAPTER NINE

I walked out of the classroom and groaned.

Jackson held out his hands. "Just hear me out."

Used to doing what I was told, I stopped. "I need to get to my next class."

"Then let me walk you. Please."

I glanced around uneasily. Glaring girl was stomping away. If she knew Peter . . . "Well, um, Peter might not like that . . ."

Once again, Jackson's jaw tightened, reminding me of Jemma's reaction. Had she told him how much she hated my boyfriend? How she thought he was rude to me? Controlling?

I was more than slightly freaking out here.

"Hear me out? Please?"

I nodded, slung my bag higher on my shoulder, and moved toward the staircase.

He followed, talking fast. "It just fell out, promise. I wasn't snooping, I didn't go through any of your other papers, nothing. I just gathered it all up."

At the bottom of the staircase, we burst into the overly warm sunlight, and I started sprinting across campus.

Close behind, Jackson said, "Look—"

I spun and held up my hand. The students swarming to

their next classes parted around us, and miraculously, no one ran into me this time.

Maybe Jackson needed to walk me to class more often. I promptly squeezed the life out of that thought.

"Stop. Please, stop. You don't owe me an explanation. I'm sorry for how I reacted, but I'm just so embarrassed. I hate being in debt."

He eyed me. "You mean you don't have any student loans?"

I shook my head, pouting a bit more than I meant to. "Nope. Just freaking six grand I have no idea how I'm going to get in the next three weeks."

He whistled. "And you've only got six grand left? Nice!"

He raised his hand for a high-five, and I awkwardly swatted at it. And missed. Of course.

"Down low's better." He held out his hand once more.

I shot him a shy grin and slapped his hand. Hard.

He sucked in a breath. "Ouch. Nice."

Just as a dopey grin was trying to overtake my face, I remembered class, spun, and sprinted for the farthest building across campus.

Jackson kept up. "Listen, about this contest . . . thing."

"Yeah? What is it?"

My speed made easy conversation a bit difficult.

"I'm honestly not sure. Someone keeps putting posters up about it, and the cleaning guys are feverishly taking them down. It's like admin doesn't want us to see them or something."

Now he had my attention. We reached the doors to the Golnath building, and I yanked them open to a blast of blessed AC. Florida was so stinking *hot* in April.

I pounded the elevator button with one hand and dug out my sweater with the other. I didn't have time for stairs. Not after stopping to talk for so long. And the AC would turn lethal as soon as I sat down and started shivering.

It took exactly ten minutes to get from Calculus to Photography, and that was the only time they gave us between classes.

And then freaking demerits.

I eyed the clock. One minute. Just one. If the elevator came this very second, I might make it. Maybe.

Two late demerits in one day was a hit, especially since too many of those got a student kicked out. And it was me. Walking demerit magnet. Even though I was scared of everything and did anything anyone told me.

Like I needed one more barrier to graduation.

The elevator door slid open, and I bolted inside, pressing the fifth-floor button a million, bazillion times. Jackson jumped in with me, and a few other stragglers stumbled in who had that same wild, desperate look in their eyes I'm sure I had.

None of us wanted penalties at the end of the school year.

"Freaking strict school," I muttered under my breath.

One of the students eyed me, and I clamped my mouth shut. Had I already mentioned I was a demerit magnet? No need tempting the demerit gods.

The elevator stopped at the fifth floor.

"Candace—"

I shook my head and bolted once the doors were open enough for me to be free. I ran toward my class.

Just as I was about to slip inside, Jackson grabbed my hand. Slid a flyer into it.

"Just read it. I won't bother you again, promise, but just read it."

I nodded, my eyes on the door—not willing to let them be captivated by his, because yeah, then I'd totally be late—and he let go.

I slipped into my seat just as the bell rang, then slumped over in relief. Oh my gosh, I made it.

I spared a quick glance at the flyer before shoving it deep in my bag. My eyes froze on the number there.

The 5,000 preceded by dollar signs registered as I pulled

my textbook from my bag and wrangled on my sweater. My heart skipped a beat. Maybe I would look into that.

But later. Mr. Jefferies was crazy strict for this being an elective.

And goodness knows how I hated to get into trouble.

CHAPTER TEN

Peter cornered me, waving around the same flyer Jackson had given me. "One thousand dollars. Each. Just for going."

I cocked my head. That's not what the flyer said. Huh. Maybe I'd read it wrong.

"Are you doing this?" he prodded, beside himself with greed. I mean, really, what else could it be? No sane person would agree to this.

I shook my head. "It's not worth it."

I'd finally read the stupid flyer. And had promptly thrown the stupid thing away.

Stupid was too tame a word.

"And then five thousand dollars for the grand prize!" I could've sworn dollar signs literally danced in his eyes. Literally.

I clenched my jaw harder. "I won't do it."

Peter huffed in exasperation. "Candace. Think about it. Didn't you say you had no idea how you were going to pay your tuition bill? Didn't you say you couldn't graduate without paying said bill? Didn't you say there was nothing more the school could do to help you out and you'd used up all of your scholarships and you couldn't get a loan? Hmm?"

My hands froze on the files I was busy filing. I had said all of that. In a moment of panic, I'd opened my big, fat, stupid mouth.

Of all the times for Peter to actually listen to me.

I spun on him. "And you think spending the night in a haunted house on the very night an entire family was murdered is the way to accomplish that, hmm?"

My voice trembled on the last word. Crazy as the whole stupid dare was, it happened to be the exact amount I needed.

I could tell from his stance, the excitement in his eyes—a little kid at Christmas had nothing on him—he'd sensed my hesitation. He swooped in for the kill. As he liked to do.

"Come on, baby. It's one night. You can keep your eyes closed the whole time." His arms came around my waist. "I'll be right there with you."

I rolled my eyes and pulled away, jabbing papers anywhere they fit. I hoped no one needed back editions of the college paper. Good luck finding them.

Peter followed me like the pest that he was. "Jer and Harriet will be there."

Oh, goodie. My least favorite people in the world. That made it better.

I clamped my mouth tighter. No way would I let those horribly negative words escape. I'd never hear the last of it.

He must've sensed he was losing me. "Six thousand dollars. Think of it. You can pay your bill. Graduate. Go to Acción with me debt free."

I shot him a look.

"Okay, discussion for another time. Got it. Anyway, the important thing here. Graduation. Being able to take your finals."

It aggravated me that I was actually considering this. Where were my standards? My perfectly reasonable, healthy fear of scary places?

Yep, still there and going strong.

"No way am I staying overnight at a haunted house with you or anybody else. Why don't you go without me? You know I don't do scary."

Peter rubbed his jaw and said absently, "I don't really need the money." Was he trying to convince me or himself? "Besides, the guys said you had to do it too, and I agree. Come on, it'll be so much fun!"

Of course that's what they'd said. James, Stewart, and Tyler had been trying to scare the crap out of me since the first day I'd set foot on campus. I had the best reactions, they said. Yeah, well, so what?

They were sponsoring this whole stupid mess. But where they'd gotten five grand to throw around like that, I'd never know.

I speared Peter with a glare. "Why? Why do they need me there so freaking badly?"

Peter shrugged. "Beats me. They said it wouldn't be any fun without you. Plus, they like how easily you scare or how loud you scream or something."

I glared.

He raised his hands and backed up a step. "Their words, not mine."

I stepped to the 2014 shelf and shoved old editions of the school magazine away with more force than was absolutely necessary. Why did we even still have these?

"How on earth can they just throw away five grand like that? Don't they have bills to pay?" My hands paused. "Will they even pay us?"

Peter's grin said it all. I was weakening. Desperation would do that to a person. I clamped my jaw tight, disgusted with the idea, but he was right. I needed that money.

"Six thousand. Think of what you could do with that much money."

I raised an eyebrow, my hand perfectly happy frozen inches away from its destination—the shelf. Sweat popped up all over, and I swallowed hard, steeling myself for disagreeing with him. "I thought it was only five?"

Questioning him didn't seem to faze him—this time. "They said they'd give an extra thousand to the last person in the house come morning." His eyes widened. "Does that mean we might get seven?" He hungrily reread the flyer. "No, I think it's just six . . ."

"And if we're all left?"

Peter laughed. "Not a chance. That place is hecka scary."

My heart shot out of my chest faster than a cat whose tail got caught under a rocker. Was this what a heart attack felt like? The room was tilting every which way, and I grabbed for the shelves.

Peter cleared his throat. "Uh, I mean, we'll push them out or something. We'll make sure we're the last ones in there. Not scary at all."

Yeah, right. There was a reason most of the other students wouldn't go near the place, and I was the only one on campus who refused to watch horror movies. In other words, pretty much everyone else in the entire world was braver than me. Everyone.

I continued to archive back issues, the sum of five thousand dollars rolling around in my head. Add the extra thousand, and my bill was covered. Especially since I'd booked all those senior shots.

My head came up. "Did you deposit those checks?"

Peter looked at me, face blank. "What checks?"

"The checks I gave you the other day during your free period? The ones I asked you to deposit, and you said you would."

He frowned. "Candace, you didn't give me any checks."

My heart plummeted right through the floor. "You didn't deposit my checks?"

Peter spread his hands. "Sorry, I'm not sure what you're talking about."

My heart raced, worse than when thinking of the haunted house. "Are you kidding me? You asked where I'd gotten so much money. The ones I said I worked so hard for?"

Someone shushed us from several rows over.

I dropped my voice. "Peter, tell me you're joking."

He looked confused. "You showed me the checks, sure, but you must've forgotten to give them to me before you ran off." He shrugged. "I just assumed you'd get them to me later."

I stared at him, mouth open, close to tears. I could've sworn I'd given him those checks, but now I was doubting myself.

And if I didn't find them ASAP, I was even further behind getting the money I needed to graduate.

Peter interrupted my inner turmoil. "Well, are you going to do it? Are you going to do this one thing to get the rest of the money you need?"

I bit back my retort about the checks he'd lost. They wouldn't have covered my bill, true, but they were mine. I'd earned them. How could he have been so careless? And forgetful?

"Please . . . just check your bag. I don't have those checks anymore."

He looked uneasy. "Candace, I'd love to help you out, I would, but I don't have them." He rubbed my arms when I opened my mouth. "But for you, I'll look. Promise. Now, about the dare?"

Guess I'd have to be happy with that. Until I could tear my dorm room apart, looking for them.

My mind scrambled for another excuse. Any excuse. But now I needed that money more than ever.

My next set of paychecks came through after my bill was due. Way to fail me, three part-time jobs. Not that my measly paychecks would've covered it anyway, but still.

I couldn't graduate without that money.

My hands stilled. Could I do it? Could I face my greatest

fear—anything that fell in the horror or suspense category—and earn enough money to take me to the finish line?

I had one month left, for pity's sake. One month. Surely I could trade one night for a whole month?

If I didn't die.

Peter's voice wedged its way into my thoughts. "You could always take out a student loan."

"No!" My eyes darted around the quiet office as my voice echoed back to me louder than it had left.

My supervisor rose from her seat and gave me her infamous look. We didn't call her the General for nothin'.

I smiled apologetically and ducked around the corner, abandoning my need to file everything in order.

"No," I repeated quietly, shaking my head. I may have been the only person on planet earth who refused to get a student loan, but I wasn't budging. I wasn't even sure I *could* get one.

My parents had lost everything, and I do mean everything—house, car, every stick of furniture, the crazy-expensive cookware my mother had bought on credit, even my camera—when they'd taken out more loans, including credit cards, than they'd had any business taking. And couldn't pay back.

Now my parents were hoarders, not to mention they had terrible credit, and I wouldn't touch a loan if it were the only way I could stay in school. Which it very well might be.

That or stay overnight at the uber-creepy mansion that even the most thrill-seeking college students wouldn't go near. And they wanted *me* there.

Yeah, right.

Trouble was, the school expected to be paid, and I was out of money. In my senior year. Right before graduation. I'd already taken an extra year to earn my degree, not counting the year I worked before college.

I was twenty-three. Practically the old lady on campus. Watching my friends graduate year after year.

Okay, maybe that was overly dramatic, but you know what I mean. I couldn't afford to miss my own graduation. Again.

My savings were gone, I worked every job I could find, and the school had worked with me all they could. I fell asleep occasionally at work. My scholarships were maxed. I didn't have time to apply for more. Finals were almost here.

Peter moved close behind me, slipping his arms around me. I glanced around fervently. The General frowned upon PDA. In college. True, it was a conservative school, but my goodness, who was that strict?

I still didn't want her seeing us hugging. For shame.

"You know I'd loan you the money if I could."

I shook my head. I wouldn't take it and he knew it. Which was probably why he said it.

"But it's one night. Just one. And you can graduate. Without staying here another semester."

I searched for any other options—any—but came up blank. My heart sank. "I can keep my eyes closed?"

I could hear the smile in his voice. "The whole time."

"I'll think about it."

Peter stifled his whoop by spinning me around and giving me a wet, slobbery kiss. How did you tell your boyfriend you couldn't stand his kisses? You didn't. Sigh. After he sucked my face for three seconds too long, he pulled back, his face radiant.

"You won't regret this. I promise!"

He bolted before he could hear my response. In other words, before I could change my mind.

"I already do," I said to no one in particular.

I caught the General's glare and ducked my head, stuffing files away as fast as I possibly could. Anything to keep my mind off tomorrow.

CHAPTER ELEVEN

I slipped out of the school newsroom, thankful my shift was over. The General hadn't stopped glaring at me for Peter disrupting everything.

Had she seen our kiss? Blerg. I wouldn't wish that on anyone.

And I couldn't stop worrying about those checks.

Right outside the doors, Jer cornered me. "So, ya gonna do it?"

Oh my gosh, were they ganging up on me?

"Well, um, ah, I don't know . . ."

Peter may have taken my hesitation as agreement, but that didn't mean I'd said yes. Oh my gosh, had Peter sicced Jer on me? Just to make sure I wouldn't back out?

I edged around him, looking for an escape.

Peter's best friend, Jeremy, could be pushy. Very pushy. At least they hadn't sent Harriet, Jer's girlfriend. There might've been a catfight.

Or so I could only hope. All I managed to do when she was around was hide, and if that didn't work out, smile harder. It was a lot of work.

Jer cackled, hemming me in no matter which direction I

went. "Oh, come on! For that much money? Of course you want to do it!"

I stopped trying to get away and just stared at him. "So all my school debt will be paid off. Just like that."

Excuse me if I didn't believe him. Who paid a college student five grand for a dare?

A person who shouldn't have that much money, that's what.

He snapped his fingers. "Just like that."

"And all I have to do is stay overnight in a haunted mansion."

"Yep, that's all." His smug face was way too confident for what he was proposing.

I burst into laughter. Bending-over-my-knees, couldn't-breathe, dying-laughing laughter. It sounded even more ridiculous coming from Jer.

"Okay, Candace, you can knock it off now." He shifted uncomfortably. "People are starting to look."

I wiped my eyes. "Do you realize who you're talking to? Me? I screamed in Peter's face because he was dressed as a wolf at Cami's Halloween party. A wolf! And that was cute compared to just about every other costume there."

At least he'd insisted it was a wolf. I was still convinced the horrid thing was a werewolf.

Jer was still glancing around him, his neck a mottled red. "Yeah, I thought I was talking to someone who needed help paying her school bill. But if that's not you . . ."

He started to walk away.

Darn right that wasn't me. I turned the other way. To think that I, Candace Marshall, world's biggest scaredy-cat, would spend the night in a creepy southern plantation house where an entire family had been murdered just for some measly money . . . yeah, right.

Five grand's worth of measly money, but still. I wasn't above waiting tables.

For life.

"Wait!"

I turned, eyebrows raised at his shout.

He came back at me, hands stuffed in his pockets, sullenly looking at all the heads that had come up at his shout. It was amazing how similar he was to Peter.

"Look, you'll be perfect for this. Trust me."

I pointed to myself. Looked around me. "You still talking to me, Sparky? Cause I see a whole campus full of people who'd be better at this than I would."

He dropped his arm around my shoulder, and I stiffened. Peter wasn't going to like that . . .

Jer interrupted my not-so-subtle craning of my neck every which way to make sure my super-sensitive boyfriend wouldn't come upon us and murder us. Specifically me.

"Look, just come. You'll start your new life debt free. That's important to you or something, right? Right. So just give it a chance. It's only rumored to be haunted, no real ghosts. Promise."

No real ghosts. Like that made me feel any better. I was pretty certain I could scare the living daylights out of myself whether any ghosts were present or not. I had a talent.

He backed away. "See you there?"

I waved him off, which he seemed to take as agreement.

It so wasn't.

Day of the dare, I would be hiding in a place no one could find me, thank you very much.

CHAPTER TWELVE

I stared at the dilapidated old building, half of it sagging into a swamp on the back right side. It might have been a glorious plantation home at one moment in time, but right now, the decrepit thing just looked . . . dead.

No way was I going in there. No way.

Spanish moss dangled from the trees in warning, telling us to flee, and Cypress trees poked their bony knees through the swamp out back, mocking us. Insects screamed at us for being there, their wails otherworldly and super creepy.

I eyed the thick sludge all over the swamp and muttered, "How many alligators am I having a sleepover with, that's what I'd like to know."

Stewart held out his fist for a fist bump. "Good one, Marshall."

It wasn't even that good and he knew it.

I just looked at him. He was the whole reason I was here. He couldn't get a fist bump outta me that easily.

He grinned, hand still raised.

I sighed and gave him a fist bump.

My eyes returned to the sprawling mansion, white pillars

cracked and covered in ivy. I was gonna hurl any second now. This was the worst idea in the history of ideas.

And to add insult to injury, Peter hadn't found the checks, and neither had I. And now my roommates were miffed because I'd left a mess of hurricane proportions in my wake. And then I'd been dragged straight here.

Apparently my secret hiding place wasn't all that secret, and Peter, Jer, and Harriet had shown up to wrestle me into the car and drive straight here. Stupid no-longer-secret reading nook.

It felt like the house was mocking me.

Stewart, James, and Tyler stood off to the side, grinning like they'd won some kind of prize. Even though they stared at me, they wouldn't turn their backs on the house across from us.

Smart men.

Peter stood off to the side, embarrassed by my display of emotions.

Hey, he was the one who wanted me here. He could just deal.

Jer and Harriet stood close together, glued at the hip, taking turns peeking at the house and giggling. Then at me and giggling.

They were *sooo* not my favorite people in the world.

Another couple, one I didn't know, stood facing the house, the girl's arms crossed and posture wide in a defiant stance, and the guy looking all laid-back and cool.

He kind of reminded me of Shaggy from *Scooby-Doo*, and she looked like that chick from *Firefly*, the one who was Mal's right-hand man. Ur, uh, woman.

What was the actress's name?

Three couples, dared to spend the night for five grand—seriously, why weren't more people here for that much money? That was a fortune to a college student.

Because they were smart. And none of us were.

I buried my face in my hands and groaned.

"All right!" Stewart clapped. "Let's get this show started."

James popped out a handheld vid recorder.

All eyes, except mine, riveted on Stewart. I only spared him a quick peek before burying my face again. How about we *not* get started and say we did?

"Okay, first of all, we're going to start off by filming an intro," Stewart continued. "Just introduce yourselves, say hi, and tell us what you think's gonna happen tonight."

The red light blinked on—I knew because I was peeking through my fingers—and James shoved the camera in Tyler's and Stewart's faces. They made goofy faces like the idiots they were, then James flipped it around so he could get some camera time too.

Professional they were not. Not even a little. But at least someone was having fun here.

The camera made its rounds to everyone else, but I was still freaking out too much to hear anything that was said. Not even sure why I didn't think I'd be on there too.

"And this is our resident scaredy-cat, Candace Marshall," said Tyler, my un-favorite person in the world. "She's the only one who doesn't want to be here."

I groaned, face still buried.

"Let's hear it from the woman herself," droned on Tyler. "Candace, what do you think's going to happen tonight?"

"Yes, Candace, do tell," added Stewart unhelpfully, choking on a laugh.

Unintelligible gargles came out from behind my hands, and before I could articulate how badly I wanted them to go away —how badly "I" wanted to go away—they were prying my hands away from my face.

"What was that, Candace?" Tyler was snickering so hard, he could barely get it out.

I stared into the dead fish-eye of a camera lens and managed to say: "I think I'm going to be sick."

All three guys shot away from me as if I had in fact just hurled all over them.

I curled in on myself and moaned some more. I kind of wish I had lost my dinner. It might get me out of this.

"That's a wrap," Stewart said in a deep, fake announcer's voice.

"Think we got enough?" Tyler craned his neck to view the footage they'd just shot.

All three huddled around the camera, commenting on several places, laughing at the footage they'd gotten . . . of me.

Great. Just great.

"Perfect." Tyler whistled, sharp and loud. "Let's go inside, people!"

The three guys led the way inside. Everyone else moved toward the house, but Peter hooked his arm through mine and practically had to drag me. Okay, he had to drag me. There was no "practically" about it.

Ten steps led up to the front doors, then five steps took us down into a spacious foyer, leaving a nice little space under the floorboards for crawling things I didn't even want to think about. Who'd designed this thing? I'd kill myself every time I came home, forgetting about the steps and tumbling down them into the main room.

Especially if it were dark. Like it was going to be soon.

Jer and Harriet and the other couple dumped camping gear in the middle of the entry room. I stared at the pile. Were we supposed to bring camping gear?

"Get a load of this place!" Happy-go-lucky-super-hippie-camper dude was waaay too thrilled about spending the night with ghosts.

I so was not.

Peter promptly deposited me next to the pile of supplies, then he moved away as if he had no idea who I was. Everyone else spread out, leaving me be, but I think they knew they didn't have anything to worry about.

I was shaking too hard to run.

My eyes darted everywhere, crazily, and I took in the decrepit house.

Built as a plantation home, turned thrice into a tourist trap (what? I'd been reading Shakespeare last night . . .), and abandoned just as many times—the people who'd dropped this place like a hot potato had more sense than any of us.

Gruesome murders had taken place here. The entire family had been slaughtered, and no one knew why or by whom. And it looked just like a place bad guys would love to dump bodies.

Especially if, say, a group of stupid college students trespassed and spent the night on a dare.

I would say "just shoot me now," but I didn't want that to happen. At all.

It may not have been Halloween anymore—the second most popular night to stay in this creepy mansion—but today, April tenth, the day the entire family had been murdered, was bad enough.

Ugh! Why was I here again?

"Listen up, people!" called Tyler. "This is how it's going to go."

I glanced at Peter. I couldn't help but notice that he was edging closer and closer to the main doors.

I was rooted to the spot, too scared out of my mind to escape while the sun was still mostly up and the door wide open.

Stupid me.

James said, "You can explore, stay here, heck, I don't care what you do, but you cannot go outside until the sun comes up and we open these doors for you."

Stewart grinned. "Emphasis on us opening the doors, not you."

Huh. Sounded like they made the rules at my school too.

My teeth started to chatter. Loudly. They were chattering

so much, in fact, I couldn't believe anyone could hear these guys over me. I wish I couldn't.

Tyler thought he'd add his two cents. "Did ya hear that? Step one foot outside, and you're instantly disqualified."

Come to think of it, not sure that was even worth two cents.

"Dis-qual-i-fied," he drawled.

Disqualified. Right. Sounded like a dream. If I could move, I'd disqualify myself right now.

I rubbed my arms, but the goosebumps refused to be rubbed away. And it was a warm night in balmy Florida.

Tyler pointed to the corners of the room. "And we'll know, cause we've got these little beauties up to track your progress."

My eyes drifted to little round dots, liberally dotted around the room, a few visible in the next. Better known as: world's smallest cameras. Soon to be privy to my humiliation.

Could this get any better?

"Also a safety measure, just in case," added James.

Apparently it could.

Safety measure? Just in case? I did an about-face and headed toward the front door.

Peter was there, herding me back to the huddle.

"So they're in all the rooms, then?" I hadn't heard stoic girl speak yet. Probably should've paid attention to her name.

"Aw, man, cameras! What if I gotta take a leak?" Super-happy-hippie guy moaned.

Harriet giggled. Did she do nothing else?

James rolled his eyes. "To answer your question, Erik, the only bathroom that kind of works is the one down here, off the kitchen. But don't go into the kitchen. You'll be swimming. Literally. And I suggest you only use the bucket of water to flush in certain situations, if you know what I mean."

Peter huffed a protest.

"And to answer *your* question, Ari, yeah, little cameras in all the rooms—except the bathroom—but mostly in the big rooms." James rubbed his hands together greedily. "We hope to catch some action."

I groaned. I hated this. So much.

"Tell me again why you big, strong, handsome ghost hunters aren't staying the night yourselves?" said grumpy, stoic girl, her name already gone from my mind, I was so freaked out.

My jaw fell open. First of all, it never would've occurred to me to talk like that to these guys — never mind that they were big, strong, and handsome — but second, all three of their chests swelled a bit.

How was a girl confident enough to have that kind of an effect on a guy?

"You do realize real ghosts mess up recording devices of any kind, right?" she continued.

Wait, what? Really? Why? And how did normal people know these kinds of awful facts?

"If this were a real ghost hunt, sure," Stewart said. "But it's not. We just want to post some footage of the dare."

Online. Great. So the rest of the students I hadn't screamed at during the Halloween party could now hear me scream. Just great.

"And we're not actually ghost hunters. We just want to top the hits we got on our site last month," Tyler added.

"Yeah, people are real excited to tune in throughout the night." James bounced up on his toes.

Stewart nodded. "Even got some all-nighter viewing parties going on."

Wait, this was live? Right now? I spun to look at the cameras. All of them? How was that even possible?

Apparently someone asked that out loud, because Stewart was answering my question.

"Motion sensors. We'll see the feeds, but only the activated ones will be live."

"What if a squirrel gets in the house?" Hippie guy snickered. "Whoa, motion all over the place." He did some weird hand signals that did in fact look like a squirrel.

James gave him a flat look. "Yeah, no, we'll control the feeds."

"Then we'll edit the final cut and put it up later," Tyler added.

Harriet was looking at me, a wicked grin on her face. "I'm just looking forward to seeing how some of us handle being here all night. In the dark."

The girl I didn't know snapped her gum. "Meh. That's nothing. What about the extra thousand?"

Tyler raised his chin in my direction. "That's for her. If she can make it till the end. Kind of an incentive, you could say."

My eyes snapped in his direction, then my gaze sought Peter's. He wasn't looking at me. The thousand was only for me? Had he told them —?

No, he looked too upset by that particular tidbit to have known anything about it.

Still, I didn't know if that made me feel better or worse.

Hippie guy burst into my thoughts with more exuberance than the situation called for. "Awesome! Let's do this! Wait. Give me a time, man. I don't want to be like, 'Maybe now I should go out, or wait, now?' I don't want to mess up and come out too soon. Or stay in here a second longer than necessary."

Harriet giggled and twirled a strand of her hair, giving Erik a flirty look. Erik, like, didn't even see it. But Jer straightened and puffed out his chest, looking for all the world like he was going to punch oblivious dude over there.

Had I mentioned how much I enjoyed being around Harriet and Jer?

But stoic girl just rolled her eyes at her boyfriend, also oblivious to all the drama. "It doesn't matter, stupid. We're not getting the extra cash."

Harriet giggled again, and I cringed. For more reasons than one. Why was no one else upset about this?

"Besides, they'll open the doors for us, remember?" new girl continued.

I cleared my throat. "Why . . .?"

Everyone looked at me.

Nothing else came out. It seemed every inch of me was too scared to work. Maybe I could pass out and wake up first thing in the morning and bolt?

Stewart shrugged after the silence had grown weird. "Anyway, we set up base at my house. We'll be watching all night long."

"So if you need us," said James, "we'll only be twenty-five, thirty minutes away. No biggie."

Yeah, no biggie to *him*. I mean, really. Thirty minutes away? We could all be dead by then!

"Awesome!" That would be Jer. Though he didn't sound as sarcastic as he should've.

Stoic girl eyed the too-polished frat guys with suspicion. "How do we know you'll even pay us?"

James leveled an almost-stern stare in her direction. I was impressed. "Have I ever not done something I said I would?"

Huh. No, he hadn't.

"No." Stoic girl sighed, like it pained her to say the word.

Harriet giggled and batted long eyelashes. "How do we know you handsome men won't be trying to scare us all night?"

Jer, once again, looked like he wanted to go on a rampaging spree. The trying to make him jealous thing was getting old. His getting jealous over everything was getting old too.

Tyler snorted. "Like I'd set foot in here tonight."

I swooned. Seriously. Everything grew hazy, the ground tilted, and I was reaching for unconsciousness with everything I had. Once again, I stumbled toward the front doors.

Peter shook my arm. "Snap out of it, Candace."

When had he gotten close to me?

"I . . . just . . . need a minute." I sank onto the bottom step at the front door.

I glanced at Peter's face on the way down. Blotchy red stained his cheeks, and he edged away from me. He hadn't said a word to me the whole time until now.

I perched on the steps and rocked back and forth, my head in my hands. Footsteps came my way.

"Hey, look, if you don't want to do this . . ."

Stewart. Had to be.

A smack. "Of course she does!"

That would be Tyler.

He knelt next to me. "You've got this. I mean, sure, a family was murdered here 175 years ago, and no one knows what happened, but it's just a scary story. No such things as real ghosts, so no big deal, right?"

Like that made me feel any better.

James shoved Stewart out of the way. "What he means to say is, that's all it is. Made-up stories. From ages ago. Can you imagine the props you'll get from staying here overnight? On the night of the supposed murder?"

I lifted my head long enough to stare into his twinkling blue eyes. Too bad he was so handsome. I felt bad for hating a guy that good looking. Especially since he really was a nice guy. The jerk.

I caught Peter out of the corner of my eye. Uh-oh. Jealous alert. I buried my face back in my arms. I didn't need to deal with that, too.

James clapped me on the shoulder, nearly sending me headfirst into the foyer. "You've got this."

Stewart checked his watch. "Hey, we gotta head out."

The other guys agreed and jog-walked up the steps to the open door. "Remember no one opens this door till we do, got it?"

"Got it," echoed exactly everyone except me.

"You've got ten minutes till sundown, guys." Tyler again. "Good luck."

The doors slammed with the receding echo of finality.

I heard running footsteps and glanced up long enough to see we were three less than we'd been. I craned my neck and peeked through one grimy window. The guys were booking it down the long drive reclaimed by nature.

Leaving us to die.

"This is the worst day of my life," I moaned.

New girl grunted. "Suck it up and let's explore this place."

She couldn't be serious.

"Uh . . ." First time I'd heard her boyfriend—Erik, was it? —not bouncing-happy over something. "What's the rush? We do have ten minutes, after all."

Jer, who stood close to the door, nodded. Come to think of it, Harriet and Peter were hovering near the front door too.

Peter stalked past us all with an exaggerated swagger. "I'm not scared of some crumbling plaster and dust. Let's get in there and conquer this place."

New girl trailed him, looking all the world like she was going to war. Harriet clamped on to Jer's arm and, yep, giggled as she followed.

I was just going to stay here, thank you very much.

Hippie dude stuck out his hand. "Erik, with a K." He hooked a thumb over his shoulder. "The warrior chick over there's mine."

I didn't bother looking. That description would never match Harriet.

I could barely get my throat to work. "Candace." I took his hand.

"Ooh, the screamer." Erik hauled me to my feet and handed me a flashlight. "Come on. You've got this."

I attempted a smile, because I absolutely was going to kill whoever had called me that, and let him drag me across the foyer.

What was a measly five thousand dollars compared to my life? And what if we all stayed in here all night long. Would we split the five grand? I had no idea.

All excellent questions to have asked before I got myself into this mess.

I eyed the steps I'd just vacated. My teammates somehow knew I was ready to bolt and hemmed me in on all sides. They dragged me away from our only way out as the warm light dimmed to shades of blue.

We were doomed.

CHAPTER THIRTEEN

As the sun continued its trek below the horizon, new girl clicked on a lantern, and she and Erik grabbed flashlights.

I seriously needed to pay attention the next time someone mentioned her name.

The brave two of our group scattered, chatting about the original wood floors, banisters, and paneling. How beautiful it would be restored.

If only the back portion of the house wasn't slowly sliding into a swamp.

"Hey, Ari, you still have that map I made?" Erik called.

Ari! That was warrior chick's name. I said it a million times under my breath, trying to memorize it. I was terrible with names.

She wordlessly took it out of her bag and handed it to him.

Jer and Harriet, still glued at the hip, were now taking selfies and making faces for the cameras, pretending to be scared. Peter, who hadn't gone far for all his bravado, was looking a little green, and I was standing by the sleeping bags, shivering.

There would be no sleeping tonight, let me tell you.

I finally made myself be brave enough to look around at the place I was spending the night. Before all daylight was gone.

Because then my eyes were staying closed, no matter what.

The foyer opened into a horseshoe shape of sorts, and would've been crazy impressive had the entire top floor not been sagging down and nearly touching the ground floor we were standing on.

My eyes traced the three stories of railings surrounding the foyer, and my heart dropped a little more with every gaping hole or missing piece of railing. I hoped we were sticking to the ground floor.

My eyes took that in too. The two hallways sprouting off on either side had chunks of cave-ins from floors above, blocking the way. The only safe-looking door was straight back, across from the front doors, though I doubted any part of this house was safe.

What'd happened anyway? Had a nuclear bomb gone off, and the outside of the plantation had somehow missed it?

"This is amazing!" Erik was bouncing around, testing everything, leaving a trail of crumbling plaster in his wake. "With Rutherford Hall's two modern renovations, I can't believe so much of the original material still exists!"

Yeah, in pieces.

Harriet stood with her hands propped on her hips, lip curled. "This is disgusting. Seriously, isn't this a huge liability?"

I snorted. "Yep, definitely. Might want to take that up with the ghosts."

Harriet shot me a glare. I already knew she didn't like me, but yikes. Maybe I should keep my mouth shut from now on.

Then a cat-like smile suffused her face, and I kinda wanted to drop through the floor. I glanced around. Uh, actually, no, not really. I'd probably end up in a bog with alligators and zombies or something.

"So. I hear Jackson walked you to class the other day."

Peter's head jerked up. Yep, the guy halfway across the building, pretending to clear rubble from in front of a blocked-off hallway. The one who hadn't acknowledged my existence since I'd embarrassed him.

"He what?" His voice came bouncing across the room.

I rolled my eyes. "Thanks a lot," I muttered to Harriet.

She winked and went back to making duck lips at her phone while everyone else explored.

I glanced at Peter, thought about explaining, then glanced away. Not my problem. My problem was being dragged into this whole mess in the first place.

"Okay, so we don't have much daylight left," said Ari, "so we need to find a safe place to camp."

As if that were even possible in this place.

Jer pointed at the floor. "I say we make base camp right here. Then we'll be ready whenever they open the doors for us."

"I say we just use those suckers right now and leave," I muttered under my breath.

"Dude, dig!" Erik pointed at the pile of rubble Peter was standing in front of. "My map says the ballroom's that way, and it's one of the only intact rooms in this dump." He squinted at the paper. "Or is that the room completely submerged?"

Erik turned the map several ways before pointing my way.

"Still got that light? It's about to get real dark up in here." Erik whistled eerily, trying to mimic a ghost.

Stupid, freaking ghosts.

My hands shook so much, I dropped my flashlight. Twice. So I tried to be helpful and turn on the rest of the emergency lights, but I couldn't get those to work either.

Ari huffed, stomped my way, and after she'd turned them on and set them on the floor, shoved my flashlight back in my hands.

The light danced all over the walls as I shook for everyone to see how scared I was. Not that they hadn't already known.

"Wait for it!" Erik held up his watch and used his fingers to count down. "Five, four, three, two, and—"

He pointed toward the window facing the sunset, and all yellow light blinked away.

"It's showtime," said Erik in a deep, creepy announcer voice.

A keening sound, like a low moan with high whistles, started far away and swept toward us. Everyone stilled.

"W-w-what's th-th-that?" I asked bravely.

Okay, it sounded braver in my head.

It rose to a piercing shriek and swirled around us, whipping out of the room with the force of a gale.

At least everyone else was now as frozen as I was, feeling a smidgeon of the terror I'd been feeling all day, as any person in their right mind should be.

Something slammed far away. *Slam, slam, slam.* The sound barreled toward us, one slam right after the other.

I flinched with each percussion.

The sound came right up to the foyer—and a metal sheet slammed over the window closest to the wall. Then the next. And the next.

The front doors . . . they were next.

We jolted into motion at once.

Peter sprinted my way—a part of me melted. How sweet of him to come to me when I needed him most.

Then he blazed right past me and hurled himself through the front doors, knocking Jer and Harriet out of the way, just as two large metal sheets shot out of the walls and slammed over the wide-open door with a resounding *boom.*

Jer and Harriet sprawled on either side of the door, looking dazed.

I ran into it. The two behind me ran into me seconds later. Jer and Harriet stared after Peter with mouths parted, faces too shocked to react—probably exactly how I looked.

I rattled it, just to be sure. It wouldn't budge.

"He left us!" Ari said, her voice brimming with disgust.

The rest of the windows in the room slammed shut in succession, choking us with dust.

"He pushed me," wailed Harriet. "Did you see that?"

I had. I'd seen him run past me and right out that door, too. And I couldn't believe it.

I clawed at the metal sheeting, but nothing.

We were trapped.

CHAPTER FOURTEEN

We all looked at each other. The final window in the room slammed shut, and the noise continued on through the house.

We bolted as one, trying to get ahead of the noise, trying to find a window or door still free to open.

The slamming accelerated.

We chased the noise, tried to get ahead of it, but everything was sealed off by the time we got there.

Erik headed toward the back right corner of the house, the only place we hadn't heard the crashing metal shutters yet.

The floor started slanting, but it didn't really make it to our brains with how panicky we all were. His foot splashed in water. And he slipped.

"Wait!" Ari hauled him back. "The swamp, remember?"

My heart sped up even more. Would the house decide to go all the way in? While we were trapped inside? Oh my gosh, could there be alligators *inside* this house?

Clinging to each other, we all backed up the slick boards till it leveled out again.

"Hey, princess, you have that flashlight?" Ari demanded.

It took me a moment to realize she was speaking to me. I glanced down at my empty hands. "N-n-n-o-o-o . . ."

"I think she dropped it near the sleeping bags" was Harriet's not-helpful comment.

And how could she even know that? She was running and screaming as much as the rest of us.

"Okay, new plan," continued Ari. "Let's go back to the bags, gear up, and find the heck outta this place."

I could get behind that plan.

We moved as one, all pressed tightly together, back the way we'd come. Dust settled around us, and crumbling plaster trickled down every once in a while from one of the newly barred windows, making me jump Every. Single. Time.

It took a while to find with the tangle of rooms we'd just run through, but we finally made it back to the front room.

Our stuff was where we'd left it.

"Oh, thank God!" I breathed out on a sigh of relief and rushed for Peter's bag. In it I found a flashlight, headlamp, and lantern. I turned them all on.

Hey. It was dark in here.

"She speaks!" The joke was halfhearted, and Erik's voice shook a little.

I didn't even attempt a fake laugh. That should prove right there how scared I was.

I always felt the need to laugh at lame jokes so the joke-teller's feelings wouldn't get hurt. Right now I was too worried about my whole body being hurt.

We all fiddled with our stuff, gearing up, taking longer than was strictly necessary since we feared we had nowhere to go and nothing to do other than be terrified out of our minds.

Just typical haunted house stuff.

Ari walked over to one of the windows and inspected it.

"Hurricane shutters?" Erik asked.

"Yep." Ari shoved at it, yanking and rattling the metal sheet. It wouldn't budge. "Good ones, too."

"So, uh, the ghosts locked us in?" Jer barked a laugh.

Ari didn't miss a beat. "Seems that way."

Jer paled, and Harriet immediately latched on to him, bottom lip trembling.

I looked around for someone to latch on to. Oh that's right. I was on my own.

Erik pointed at one of the round dots on the wall. "Or someone on the other end of those cameras is laughing at our expense."

Ari jerked her head. "Come on. Let's find a way out."

Jer hung back. "What, uh, what about the money?"

She gave him an irritated look. "I didn't say we had to leave. But do you want to be trapped in here all night, especially if things get worse?"

I shook my head just as hard as Harriet and Jer. Maybe harder.

"Didn't think so." Without another word, Ari stalked off.

I trailed everyone as we searched the entire house, but there wasn't one window or door that didn't have a metal hurricane shutter over it. Upstairs was too wrecked to even attempt getting up the shattered staircase.

What the actual heck?

About half an hour later, we found ourselves back in the foyer.

"So what now?" Erik asked.

Ari looked like she was trying to puzzle it out. "Maybe we should split up and—?"

Harriet spoke up. "Excuse me?"

I blurted the first thing that came to me. "We're sticking together."

Both guys nodded enthusiastically.

Ari sighed, like she couldn't believe she'd been stuck with such morons. "Fine."

"Besides," Erik said. "This'll be great for my paper on Rutherford Hall's mysterious past."

Jer crossed his arms. "What exactly happened here anyway?"

Erik's eyes glowed, like literally glowed, and he launched into a monologue that was actually somewhat interesting, considering it was a history lesson on steroids.

"So this place was built in the 1840s by the Rutherford family not long after Spanish settlers were run out of this part of Florida. They were one of the wealthiest families in the area, owning over 2,000 acres and roughly 300 slaves. Mr. Rutherford designed this house from scratch, and although they were known as a good, upstanding, Christian family in the community, rumors abounded over their mistreatment of their servants, Mr. Rutherford's affairs, and Mrs. Rutherford's temper."

My eyes started to glaze over. Did I say this was interesting? I take it back.

Erik sucked in a breath, ready to launch into the next phase of the history of Rutherford Hall.

Jer held up a hand. "Yeah, look. I didn't know that was going to happen. Never mind."

Harriet's eyes were all glazed over too. She shook herself out of it and flipped her hair over her shoulder. "Well, I for one want to know nothing about that night. It was stupid and has nothing to do with us."

Erik's face fell, and I instantly felt sorry for the dude. He'd been nothing but nice since I'd met him.

I jumped in. "How do you know so much about this place?"

Erik puffed out his chest. "History-anthropology double major. I'm getting my master's in archaeology next."

Ari gave him a glowing look that totally didn't match her words. "Which pretty much makes him the most boring person on earth."

He grinned back at her. "You know it, baby."

I stifled a groan. Did everyone on the planet have a better relationship than me? And how was that kind of conversation even used for flirting?

Erik draped his arm around his girlfriend's shoulders. "What's the plan, mermaid-mine?"

Ari turned all business, though her cheeks went pink. "I say we lay out our sleeping bags and try to get some shut-eye."

Like that would happen at any time tonight.

And shut-eye? Who talked like that? Girl thought she was in a western, not a horror movie.

Erik blew out a breath. "As long as I get the middle."

"What? Nooo!" I wailed.

He lifted his hand and feebly laughed. "Just kidding, just kidding." He pointed at me with both hands. "But I got you to speak again. Boo-yah!"

I didn't know what to make of weirdo over there, so I just looked at him.

Ari gave me an irritated look. "We'll give sleeping beauty here the middle for now, but no crying or shaking or any of that other stuff you've got going on or you're out, got it?"

I nodded too many times, then licked my lips. Hope flickered like a flame fighting madly for its life. "Like, um, outside?"

She rolled her eyes. "No, stupid, or we'd all be out there."

"Hey, there's no call for that," hippie dude objected.

Ari turned away and grumbled.

Erik gave me an apologetic look and took two steps away to lay out his bed for the night. Jer and Harriet looked like they didn't want to, but they started laying out their sleeping bags as well.

Ari still looked disgusted with me.

And I decided to make nice since I'd been clutching her arm and screaming in her ear for the last hour or so and had to spend the night next to her. I searched for something to say, and the first thing I could think of popped out before I could stop it.

"So, um, I never did catch your name."

I almost smacked my forehead. I mean, really? I'd only been trying to memorize her name all night!

Her mouth tightened, but I couldn't understand why.

Her answer was short, curt. "Arielle."

My jaw dropped. "But you, he, your boyfriend . . ."

"You say one word about it, and I'll punch that winey, sniveling mouth of yours until you forget we even have names."

My mouth snapped shut, my eyes ten times their normal size.

"That's what I thought." She marched away, grabbed a lantern, and started fiddling with it.

Geez Louise. Angry much?

Erik leaned close with a conspiratorial grin and a wink. "She wouldn't really, you know. Punch you."

I looked after her. "Wouldn't she?"

He looked uncertain for a moment, then shrugged. "Maybe. But I doubt it. Just call her Ari and you're good."

Well wasn't that just a relief. I grabbed the remaining sleeping bag. Probably Peter's.

The jerk.

We laid out our bags, the girls sandwiched Peter's sleeping bag between theirs, and we unzipped them for easy escape—at least, that's why I unzipped mine—and laid back under the dusty chandelier.

"Uh," I said.

"Way ahead of you, sunshine," Ari snapped.

All eyes riveted on the spiky ball of death over our heads, we inched our little camp closer to the front door. No way were we going *farther* into the house . . .

"Are you sure you guys don't want to explore more?" Ari asked.

"No!" the rest of us said at the same time.

CHAPTER FIFTEEN

After about an hour or two of not sleeping and every creak turning into nothing more than a regular old sound, I tried to relax my clenched muscles. All of them. I was in major pain. And I had to pee.

Not happening this night, let me tell you.

I slowly pointed my toes. Unclenched my fists. Stretched my neck. And let out a deep sigh. Maybe we would survive this night after all.

A tremendous crescendo, as loud as a thunder crash, sent me screaming to my feet.

It was hard to tell over the volume, but I was pretty sure my companions were screaming too. We were certainly holding each other tightly enough.

The throbbing noise continued, changing in pitch and key, rattling our bones and the floorboards under our feet.

This was it. Not only would we be deaf for life, the sound was going to rattle the rest of the house right into the swamp. Goodbye, world.

I tried to cover my ears with my shoulders, but it didn't work. But no way was I letting go of the very real human arms clutching mine.

My headlamp was gone. Lanterns kicked over and broken. Our flashlights pointing in each other's faces.

Super helpful.

The noise snuffed out. Our screaming, not so much.

"All right, all right!" Ari finally shouted.

Harriet whimpered. Jer and Erik and I stopped screaming, but we still clutched each other and shook. No one was taking that basic human right away from me.

"Think it was the organ?" Ari asked.

Erik and I looked at her dumbly.

"What organ?" he finally shouted, right in her face.

"Uh, only the one we ran past a dozen times, remember?" Ari gave him a "duh" look.

"No!" Erik shouted, close to hysteria. "I wasn't looking at the furniture while I was trying to escape with my life!"

Ari rolled her eyes. "All I'm saying is we should go look for it. It's probably stuck on or something."

That was my exact rational thought too. Not.

"All it is? All it is?" Erik was close to hyperventilation. "Oh, sure, let's go look for it, she says. Well, I'm not going anywhere! I'm staying right here until they get back and let us out of here."

"And I say we figure out what kind of prank those guys are playing on us instead of sitting here wetting our panties!" Ari shouted right back at him.

I was wholeheartedly agreeing with every shouted word. Of Erik's. Not Arielle's.

It was killing me that I couldn't make a joke about their names.

"I'm not going to—"

"Well, if you're going to be a baby about it—"

"What if we just—"

Harriet started sobbing. Although I wanted to join her, I wasn't sure if that was worse or better than the giggling. Jer just looked like he was having trouble functioning.

I couldn't blame him.

A chill swept the room, and all of us froze, sentences left dangling. My breath puffed out in a cloud of fog, and I officially freaked out.

It was summer. In Florida. Warm, balmy, humid Florida.

A blue light appeared and swelled in the doorway to our right, directly across from the front door.

I didn't want to look. I really didn't. But my eyes were drawn to the pulsing blue light in the doorway leading to the rest of the house.

The light just hovered there, and I very much felt like it was staring back.

With another crash of noise from the organ, rubble lifted itself off the floor and rebuilt itself into a gleaming, beautiful plantation home. Blue light blazed in sconces on the wall, vibrant colors replaced gray, dusty tones, and furniture that hadn't been there before revealed itself in ghostly shades of blue.

I immediately used Erik and his girl as human shields. Jer and Harriet pressed themselves close at my back. Surrounded was good. The only good thing about this place.

The sprawling staircase the blue light illuminated might have been impressive if not for the blue light itself. It coalesced into a person who stood there, staring at us.

It came from a freaking ghost.

A ghost.

Did anyone hear me? A. *Ghost*. I could hardly form a thought with all the screaming my brain was doing at the moment.

Not cool.

"The master will see you now."

Erik and I let out the same high-pitched, little-girl scream at the same time. Harriet cried harder. And Jer stared with his mouth hanging open, a dazed look in his eyes.

It didn't faze the ghost in the least. He beckoned us

forward with a gloved hand, butler livery pressed neatly in place, then turned and walked into the giant room behind him, lighting the way as he went.

"Can the two of you stop screaming long enough for us to come up with a plan? K, thanks." Ari huffed out a breath.

I looked at Ari. Had she lost her mind? "A plan?"

Erik may have been shaking harder than I was. "What, like not dying before morning?" He took a step toward a mounted camera. "Are you happy now, huh? I hope you got that, because as soon as you jokers let us out, there's going to be a new murder at Rutherford Hall!"

"Way to admit that on camera," Ari muttered.

Erik was close to losing it, big time. Me? I'd lost it a while ago. I was just better at keeping it in.

I was laughing at that one too.

"Okay, so . . ." Ari looked to me for some reason. "I guess we follow it?"

I shook my head desperately no, but she was already pulling the three of us forward, Jer and Harriet clinging to me, all of us clamped together in one big cluster.

I wasn't letting go of my human shields.

Dark shapes darted in and out of my vision from the corners of the room, but every time I shined a light on them, they were gone.

I may have helped Ari drag the others after the ghost we could actually see.

We stepped into the vast room with a sweeping curved staircase, a large organ, and a table and chairs that swept the length of the room. It was massive. Were there even enough guests near this secluded plantation home back in the day to surround this table? There had to be, like, over fifty chairs.

The ghost waited for us at the top of the stairs, right before it curved out of sight. "The master will see you now."

How had he gotten up there so quickly? Besides being, well, a ghost. My face flamed at the inane question.

That was talent right there, getting embarrassed over the conversation I was having in my head.

"The master will see you now."

"I really hope he has another phrase than that," said Ari.

"Me too," Erik agreed.

"But do we really?" I asked.

They both looked at me. I looked back. No one had anything to say to that. Not even the quivering mass of two at my back.

We moved on, past the table, toward the stairs, as the ghost beckoned us to follow.

CHAPTER SIXTEEN

Apparently we weren't moving fast enough for the ghost. He beckoned harder as we inched toward the steps.

"The master will see you now," he insisted.

I froze at the base of the stairs, clutching Erik's and Ari's arms, unable to take another step. What if the reconstructed staircase was just an illusion? What if we got halfway up and plummeted to our deaths?

"Um, guys? I can't move," I whispered.

The image on the staircase flickered.

Jer barked a laugh. "Ha! He's just a projection, see? Based on the angle of the light, there should be a projector there, there, and here. See?"

He jogged up the steps—the now-solid steps, I would like to emphatically point out—and waved his hand in front of one of the cameras, but nothing. He craned his neck and glanced around. Then he prowled a bit, searching, walking through the ghost a few times. He shivered and rubbed his arms.

"Huh. They've got to be somewhere around here."

The temp in the room dropped like crazy, and air left my mouth in a puff of fog. Again. It was freaking April! In Florida. Stinking hot Florida.

How were they not getting all the ways this wasn't good?

Disdain dripped from the butler's words and upturned nose. "The master will see you now."

We all bunched together and huddled our way up the stairs, willingly going to our deaths.

I glanced down. The missing portion of staircase, now covered in ghostly blue, was solid under my feet and felt somewhat like a glass pane. The color rippled a little. I jerked my gaze away.

I wasn't entirely thrilled about staring through the floor I was walking on. And my mind couldn't even begin to comprehend how that was possible.

We followed him down one of the previously mutilated hallways, still huddled in a cluster.

Jer craned his neck, trying to figure it out. "There should be projectors. We should see the light turn and pass from projector to projector as we pass them."

He sounded less sure by the second.

Harriet attempted a laugh, but it died a quick death in her throat.

The butler led us into one of the rooms and stepped back, letting us look our fill. I darted quick, nervous glances around the room, not taking my eyes off the ghost for more than a second.

The gutted room was dancing with blue images of frilly furniture, a rocking horse, and a creepy doll the size of the rocking chair it was draped over. I didn't need the dollhouse in the corner to tell me this was previously a little girl's room.

What I needed someone to tell me was what the heck we were doing here.

He pointed at Harriet—she blanched white—then pointed at the room. Whatever the ghost was trying to say was lost on his terrified audience. Then he turned his back to us and drifted through the door that had swung shut behind us.

I blinked. The door had shut? When had that happened?

Erik threw open the door, and all five of us competed for who could get through it at the exact same time. I was squeezed to the back, of course, but I managed to get through with only a few scrapes.

The ghost was waiting for us in the hall. I drew up short, not expecting him for some reason. I was hoping he'd left. For good.

Could this be over yet?

He led us to the next room, and we repeated the same process. Well, this time Ari made sure the door stayed open, standing guard like the warrior she was.

I wanted one ounce of her bravery. Just one.

I threw a glance around the room he pointed out. This time it looked like twin boys had shared a room. Everything was duplicated and boyish, and I couldn't care less. I felt like I was politely viewing a collection saved by an eccentric hoarder, where I had to pretend to be interested.

But no rest for the weary. The ghost relentlessly marched us on. The five of us moved as one after him, too scared to do anything but obey.

The ghost drifted down the hall, then turned and gestured at the door at the end of the hall. Which meant to get past him, we would have to walk through him.

"Do we really need to go in there? Really?" I squeaked.

"What she said," Erik added.

The ghost pointed one long, bony finger, not accepting our hesitation.

Apparently we did.

I hung back, but everyone else pressed past him and into the third room, so I went along with the crowd. I certainly wasn't staying in that hall by myself. I squeezed my eyes shut as I glided past him, clutching whoever's hand was closest.

A pocket of cold air drifted by me, and I was beyond thankful when I couldn't feel it anymore.

"Whoa," breathed Ari. "That's amazing."

"You said it," agreed Jer.

"I'd kill to have this bedroom!" Harriet squealed.

I wanted to smack her and tell her never to say such things around a ghost, but I wasn't functioning at the moment.

"The historical detail is incredible!" Erik, who else?

I was going to have to look, wasn't I? I peeked out of one eye, then the other.

The most gorgeous plantation master bedroom stood in half-solid, half-ghosted lines before us, positively indecent in its decadence.

"Dude!" I said.

Four heads swiveled my way, and I shrugged even as my face burned.

"What? I'm from California. People say that there." Even if I'd never been surfing in my life.

Erik, the history buff, couldn't contain his excitement. "Get a load of this place!"

Then he launched into another of his most boring history lessons ever, which I mostly blocked. Something about where the materials came from and the innovations the Rutherfords insisted on installing in their home, which made the plantation well ahead of its time, and how it was such a shame it had fallen into disrepair.

And something about how the home had been renovated several times, by private owners and those wanting to turn it into a tourist trap, but they'd been run out every time—by something vengeful and unseen.

Again, I wasn't really paying attention. I was too busy being impressed by the place.

I mean, really, how could anyone afford such opulence, remembered or real?

Three words from Erik's lesson jumped out at me: "plantation," "cotton," and "owners."

Oh, right, plantation home. Built on the backs of slave labor.

Suddenly I wasn't so impressed.

"The master will see you now."

We all turned toward the ghost, and terror swept me afresh. Couldn't he just leave us alone already?

If a ghost could look irritated, he certainly was. What had we done to offend the dead dude?

He gestured harder, taking a moment to look at a timepiece in his suit's breast pocket. "The master will see you now?"

"Okay, okay, don't get your panties in a twist. We're coming," groused Ari.

"But do we have to?" moaned Harriet.

Hey, at least I wasn't the only one scared out of my mind.

"But—but—history needs to remember this place! There are no surviving pictures. Just a few of the family, and those are mostly damaged." Erik scrabbled for his phone, which kept slipping out of his fingers.

Ari plucked it out of the air after he'd missed catching it about five times. She swiped the phone to life and flipped the screen around so we could all see it. "See? No reception. No screen. No camera. Ghosts mess with devices, I'm telling you."

Erik's phone popped and fizzed and made screechy noises that had us all cowering away from it. And the screen stayed decidedly blank with these weird lines traveling through it in waves.

Just great. I hoped those three jokers were on their way right now to rescue us from this place. I suddenly remembered I'd forgotten my phone and was thankful I had. Especially if ghosts did any lasting damage.

Ari clicked it off and handed it back to him. Erik's face fell, and although he clearly didn't want to leave, Ari grabbed his arm and dragged him out anyway.

We followed the ghost down two more hallways, where he stopped and opened a door.

Even though it wasn't possible, we huddled tighter together.

He took us into a sitting room and left us there.

"Oh, crap." Erik's mood shifted, and now he was quaking like an earthquake. "Did y'all notice what rooms he took us to?"

Harriet and I shook our heads in unison.

He dropped his voice to a scared, shaky whisper. Only this time, he wasn't trying to scare us. He was truly, actually scared.

Not something I wanted to think about at the moment.

"The ones the family were murdered in. That night."

The room grew kind of hazy and blinked out for a moment. Or maybe that was just me. "Um, what?"

"Yeah."

I couldn't stop myself from asking. "And this room?"

He shook his head. "Nothing happened in this room, not that I remember."

I cocked my head. "You really do know everything about this place, don't you?"

His grin was severely lacking its usual exuberance. "Yeah."

Cold wind swept the room, and moaning, groaning, keening—in other words, every ghost noise imaginable—swirled around us as we huddled there, quavering in our boots.

Who said being scared was fun? I was going to kill him.

"H-how can it be so c-c-cold in Florida?" Jer stuttered.

Ari and I looked at him at the same time.

"Have you never been in an air-conditioned building here?" Ari demanded.

"Yeah, they try to freeze our butts off in the entire state. How is this new to you?" Harriet added, some of her spark returning.

"Th-this feels c-c-colder," Jer insisted.

I hated to admit it, but he was right. Bone-jarring cold settled into our bones and made the air poof with fog around our breaths—worst day ever. I'd take twenty-degree air conditioning over this any day.

One by one, doors started slamming all up and down the hall. All of them, not just the three rooms we'd looked in, but my goodness, why? *Why?*

We bunched closer as the noises grew louder, building up to something.

Our door crashed open, and the rest of the door slamming fell silent. We all jumped, and I yelped, as our ghost guide stood framed in the doorway.

"The master will see you now."

CHAPTER SEVENTEEN

No one budged.

The ghost waved the way, looking excited now, but we all just stood there. Did we really want to follow him? I mean, really?

"M-m-maybe we d-d-don't want to see the m-m-master," I stuttered out, scared out of my mind. Who had been slamming all those doors?

You know what? I didn't want to know.

He beckoned harder, his brow lowering in a dark frown. I tried not to look at him as we moved as one out the door and back down the staircase.

"So tell us everything," Harriet said to Erik.

Jer arched an eyebrow in her direction. "I thought you didn't want to know anything about that night. That it was stupid and had nothing to do with us."

Harriet rolled her eyes. "Well now it obviously does, dimwit."

I nodded, over and over again.

Erik shook his head. "It's only conjecture. No one really knows what happened."

"Tell us anyway," Jer demanded.

"Yeah, if we're walking to our deaths, I kind of want to know what's going to happen to us," Ari agreed.

Walking to our deaths. Did she really have to say that out loud?

Erik sighed, as if pained to relay such inaccuracy. "They think Mrs. Rutherford found her husband in the midst of an indiscretion. She then retrieved his hunting musket and went on a killing spree, murdering everyone in the house that night, even her children and then herself. No one got out, so no one knows what really happened. Just that everyone died. There had been a few altercations already, according to the servants, because she suspected a few of the servant's children were her husband's."

I shuddered. "I like the guy already."

They all looked at me.

"You know I'm kidding, right?"

Erik kept talking. "He was a violent man, prone to using his fists, and gossip said the Mrs. wasn't quite herself after having children. They think latent postpartum depression, not diagnosed at that time and getting worse with age."

I glanced all around me as we moved down the stairs, through the foyer, and toward the ornate dining room. "And it had nothing to do with her creep of a husband. Right."

I got funny looks again—I hated that they kept doing that—and we walked into the ornate dining room.

"And she, er, uh . . ." Erik pointed. "She's right there."

We all froze. The entire family stood around the table, behind their chairs, apparently waiting for us. *Us.*

A beautiful little girl, twin boys, and a man at the head of the table with a handlebar mustache, complete with a young deranged-looking woman next to him, all turned their specter eyes our way and left them there.

Could I emphasize in how many ways this wasn't good?

Erik sucked in a breath. "Oh my giddy aunt."

I looked at Erik. Had to admit, I'd always wanted to meet

someone who actually said that. Not what I expected my last fulfilled wish on earth to be, though.

"It's them." Erik continued. "Exactly. I mean, exactly, exactly. Only a few old tintypes remain, but they nailed it. This is like a history lesson on steroids!"

Some of his exuberance was starting to trickle back in.

Ari glared at him. "Yeah, but the last people who stayed here on this night kinda ended up dead. Not exactly what I want to happen to us."

Erik shook himself out of it. "Right, uh, you're right."

Jer went pale faster than Harriet had earlier. "They what? They *died*?"

"And why are we finding this out now?" Harriet wailed.

One thing was certain: I now knew why college students weren't lining up at the doors for this dare. I did an about-face and headed toward the kitchen.

Guess I was swimming out. With the alligators. And anacondas. And whatever other giant thing wanted to eat me.

Ari hauled me back this time. "Marshall, don't do anything stupid."

I looked at her like she'd lost her mind and pointed at the ghosts. "More than being here? With them?"

She gave me a hard look. "We're getting out of this. I don't know how, but we're getting out of this. Just stick with me."

I wanted to believe her, I did, but ghosts were speaking to us and giving us tours of their mansion and expecting us for dinner and stuff. Swimming with deadly things was pretty much the better option here.

"Please, dinner is served."

We all jumped as the wife spoke, her voice rich, full, deep. She was so young looking, in an ethereal white dress, dark hair curling gently over her shoulders. Why had she married such an old dude? My eyes drifted to him as she waved us toward the chairs.

He had to at least be in his forties.

We moved as one toward the chairs. One of us may have been dragged. We stopped and stared at a single chair.

"I, uh, don't think we'll all fit in one chair . . ." I started.

"Well then clearly we'll have to sit in separate seats!" Ari snapped.

None of us moved.

The family took their seats and stared expectantly at us while Mrs. Rutherford kept standing. "Please," the wife said again, waving a hand at six empty chairs scattered around the table, "dinner is served."

We slid into seats directly next to each other—not exactly where we'd been told to sit—then scooted them as close as possible to each other.

"Now, dinner is served." The wife stood tall and clasped her hands.

Her children and husband remained eerie spectators. Guests, many, many guests, streamed to their seats in trails of blue and sat at the table.

One sat in Jer's chair, and I thought he was going to have a stroke right then and there as the plump lady tore into the ghostly food on his plate.

He infinitesimally leaned toward Harriet, chin trembling. "She's . . . so . . . cold . . ." His teeth underscored his words with a loud chatter.

Then the specters melted away, and couples danced all over the giant room, around and around and through the tables. Which kinda looked familiar, but I was too freaked out to remember from what.

A chill swept by with each pass, but nothing else in the room moved. Not the tablecloth made of blue light, not our real cloths, hair—nothing.

Then they all had their coats and were streaming to the side of the room, getting into ghost carriages and departing.

I pressed my back so hard into my chair, I was pretty sure the thing was going to topple over any second now.

I leaned toward Erik. "Where's the panic button again?"

He didn't answer me, just kept staring at the ghost hostess, her eyes roving over the table and each of us in turn.

Her vacant eyes rested on me, and I almost died. "Dinner has been served."

I slapped the table and stood. "That's it. I'm done."

My chair fell to the ground, and I jumped over it as I bolted.

And the floor dropped out from beneath me.

CHAPTER EIGHTEEN

Screaming. So much screaming. And for once, it wasn't just me.

Not that I was overly thrilled about that little fact. I was too busy doing important things like screaming.

I landed in a completely dark room, with something scratchy like hay all over the dusty wooden floor.

"Shh!" Ari hissed.

Erik and I stopped screaming the moment we found each other and clung on for dear life.

Ari huffed. "Seriously, can you guys come over here? Follow my voice."

I shook my head furiously—like she could see that in the pitch black—and Erik's trembling voice said what I wanted to say but couldn't get out.

"M-maybe y-you should-d come th-this w-way . . ."

Ari huffed some more—I was positive she was rolling her eyes—and crawled our way.

Erik must've been brave enough to reach out and grab her —she was his girlfriend, after all—but I was clinging to him for all I had.

Ari wedged her way between us. "Back off, Marshall."

I made some gasping noises, trying to convey my non-interest, but pretty sure that didn't get through.

"Okay, so let's find our way out." Ari moved forward, effectively dragging us with her, and then she was gone, seconds before a splash met our ears.

The gnarly pond! I just knew we'd run into it again. Plus, alligators.

Not the best thought to have as we followed her into the nasty-smelling water.

I opened my mouth to scream, but instead tried to drown myself as water flooded my nose and mouth. Ari and Erik had the presence of mind to save themselves, then drag me out of the water and back onto the planks we'd fallen from.

"Careful, Marshall! The boards are rotten here."

"Where are we?" I gasped out between hacks. "And can I leave now?" I was shaking so hard, I was concerned there might be bruises. "Who needs five thousand dollars? I don't. I'll just—"

"Shut it, Candace." Ari sounded breathless. "I don't think this is a prank, you guys. That water was deep. Everything is just a little too . . . real."

Erik shook with the force of a hurricane. "Probably didn't want us to break anything. I still call projectors. Right, Jer? Jer?"

I gasped. "Did they drown?"

Even Ari sounded a little shaken. "I don't think they fell down here with us."

"Then we should find them. Shouldn't we find them?" Erik sounded close to some kind of a breakdown.

Hey, I was the only one allowed to have a nervous breakdown around here.

"I just want out of this whole, big, stupid mess . . . ." My voice sounded all thick and close to tears. "And Peter, he—he—he—" I choked on a sob.

Okay, I admit it. I was spiraling. And I wasn't trying too

hard to stop myself. I'd never wanted to come in the first place. And Peter had ditched me. Ditched me!

I mean, I wished I'd thought of it first, but I was too busy running around and screaming and not thinking like an idiot. He could've at least grabbed my hand as he ran by!

"Let's just focus on getting out, okay, people?" Ari started to crawl away, and I followed her, close enough to claim no personal space whatsoever.

Light suffused the room from a doorway above us, and I blinked owlishly into the glaring light. We all probably looked like total idiots crawling around on the floor like that.

The butler came into view as my eyes focused. We were in a pantry of some kind. "The master will see you now."

"Think that means he's letting us out of here?" Ari asked.

Erik nodded enthusiastically. "Quite. Absolutely. Yes."

"Then what are we still doing here?" I demanded.

We all scrambled to our feet and darted after him, ducking our heads under the low ceiling. No one wanted to get left behind. Or be last. Nope, that honor fell to me.

We scrambled up the wooden stairs, and I peeked over my shoulder into the pitch black and wished I hadn't. Just what kind of creature was waiting to grab me in the dark?

I may have pushed them a little faster up the stairs, not that anyone was complaining.

We came up out of the cellar, dripping wet, shoes squishing, and followed the butler into the main hallway. A banshee's shriek nearly made me wet my pants—nearly—and Erik knocked us to the ground as Ari and I were busy trying to figure out where it was coming from.

An ax stuck in the wall, right over our heads.

I may have started sobbing. Maybe.

The butler continued, unfazed, up the staircase, leading the way to the family's rooms. I assumed. We most definitely did not follow.

"Dinner is served!"

My head jerked toward the shout. The Mrs. looked half-crazed, her chest heaving, eyes blazing, as she faced off with her husband.

We all just lay in a heap on the floor and watched the madness unfold.

"I am master of this house."

Although what's-his-name, the husband, still looked a little shaken—I mean, who wouldn't be shaken after having an ax thrown at them?—fury overcame his features, and he advanced on his wife.

He grabbed her hair and pulled her close. She cried out but kept her glare firmly on him.

"I am master of this house."

Light flared on a ghost we hadn't noticed. Partially dressed in servant's attire, she lay on a bed, silently sobbing, her hand stretched out in silent pleading toward the wife.

The mistress looked at the servant and then away. The woman curled in on herself in despair.

"Hey," I said without thinking. "Leave her alone. Leave them both alone!"

Erik shoved me off him and darted away, probably thinking she would come after us next, thanks to me. I couldn't blame him. I wasn't far behind.

And although I swear nothing ever rattled Ari, I turned around when a wall blocked our escape, and she ran into me.

"Oh! S-sorry," I stammered.

She shoved me aside and clung to her boyfriend. I stared back the way we'd come. We hadn't been noticed, thank God.

"I am master of this house!"

The husband slammed his wife's head into the ground and stalked off, tucking his shirt into his pants and then adjusting his cravat on the way.

I wanted to help her up, I did, since that was my first reaction, to help someone in pain, but the ghostly light emanating from her and the murder in her eyes kept me firmly in place like a big, fat chicken.

Coward, thy name is Candace.

Mrs. Rutherford slowly got up, her footsteps soft as she padded over to the fireplace, lifted the hunting musket from its place, and sighted it on her husband's back.

"Watch out!" I shouted.

Too late. We all cried out and huddled closer as the loudest gunshot I'd heard in my life erupted from the weapon. Blood sprayed—the crimson the only different color than the ghostly blue—and the husband went down.

Then she aimed at the servant.

I didn't stick around.

Erik and Ari caught up with me at some point, but if there was a back door in this place, I was going to find it. Or make one. Nothing could keep me in here after that.

Panic ensued, and servant ghosts ran all around us, most falling to a spray of crimson. Most of the men ran toward the sound, while the women screamed and streamed away, leaving trailing wisps in their wake as they disappeared through walls.

Mrs. Rutherford followed them through the walls and hunted them all down.

Gunshots echoed all around us, and a faint scent of gunpowder wafted through the air. I tried every door and window we came to, but they were all the same. Completely inaccessible, metal sheeting keeping us in.

Why? *Why?* I shouldn't be here. I didn't want to be here. My jaw tightened. I was never letting Peter force me into doing something I didn't want to do, not ever again.

Gunfire sounded behind us, steady and terrifying. Maybe we could break through a wall?

"Did you notice"—Erik gasped out the words—"that she hasn't stopped to reload? Not once?"

"Does it look like I care?" Ari retorted.

"Yeah, but she has powder and buckshot. She should have to reload between every shot." He looked at me. "Yeah?"

I threw my hands out to the side, terror making a gooshy, jelly mess of me. "Do I look like I know anything about guns? She's a ghost, for pity's sake. Keep trying to find a way out!"

And we did just that.

Three loud gunshots rang out in succession, a floor right above our heads. Near the family's chambers. The sound echoed down the staircase we'd gone up earlier.

After a heart-stopping pause, the worst keening, wailing, moaning sound ever floated down next, and my heart clenched. I'd never heard such agony before.

"Nooooooo!" The word floated around us, vibrating in my chest, its sigh like a long, drawn-out sob.

Terror, my constant companion tonight, nudged me and reminded me that clawing through the kitchen door was totally an option. Erik and Ari joined me. Stupid thing was hardwood, not rotting in the least, and even though this door had no metal sheeting, it had swelled enough that it had practically become one with the doorframe.

It. Would. Not. Budge.

Erik finally stopped, and Ari and I turned to look at him. He swallowed hard. "Guys, I think we're gonna have to go the other way—back toward the foyer—if we want to find a way out."

"You mean . . ." Ari blanched white.

He nodded. "Past the crazy missus."

I shook my head and attacked the kitchen door with more fervor, water up to my shins. "No. We can get out this way. I just know it!"

Ari grabbed my arm. "Shh. Listen."

We did.

"What?" I asked.

Ari rolled her eyes. "She stopped shooting and wailing, dimwit. Maybe we can get by her?"

My eyebrows tried to scale my forehead and leave it far behind. "Are you kidding me? Do we know for a fact these bullets are made of nothing but ghost? Or can they get us too? I mean, I don't know about you, but that looked like real blood to me."

Erik's voice was a bit shaky. "This may be our only chance if she's, you know, busy somewhere else."

I glared at him. "And if she's not?"

Erik drew one finger across his neck and gagged, pretending to be dead.

Ari smacked him. "Grow up."

He grinned at her. "You know you love me."

She headed back the way we'd come, sloshing through water. "I do, and I'd like to keep you. Let's hurry." I started to protest, but Ari just looked at me. "Look, we're going to do this."

I stood there and trembled for all I was worth.

Ari sighed and held out her arm, as if giving me permission to cling to it. I didn't give her even a moment to change her mind. I grabbed that sucker and held on for dear life.

"Okay," said Erik, sounding just as shaky as I was and clutching her other arm. "Let's get out of here."

I groaned and allowed Ari to drag me after her, certain we were heading in entirely the wrong direction.

CHAPTER NINETEEN

Ari peeked around the corner first. The huge room stretched before us, staircase silent and deadly, as the room still glowed blue.

I was tasked with watching our backs, but I really wanted to know what was going on out there. And I didn't. All at the same time. I tried to see over her and Erik's heads.

"Candace! Eyes behind."

"Oh! Right. Sorry." I shot a quick glance behind us, then was somehow looking in their direction again.

Ari just rolled her eyes and went back to surveying the room. "I don't see anything. Think we're good?"

Erik shuddered. "Only one way to find out."

Ari nodded. "On my mark . . ."

"What?" I shook my head. "No way. Nope. Not gonna happen."

"Get set . . ."

"Seriously, you guys?" I huffed. Ghosts could go through floors and walls and things. And everything was so lit up with blue light already, we'd never even see her coming.

"Go!"

And they were gone.

I stared after them. They'd left me! I mean, it was kinda my fault since I was too scared to move and all, but still. Running past where the ghost lady had been shooting last was the dumbest idea ever!

Once they reached the other side of the room, Erik threw a glance over his shoulder. "Candace! Come on! Before she gets back—"

Wood paneling splintered near his head.

I screamed, he screamed, we all screamed—you get the idea. And Erik and Ari competed for a sprinting medal and headed back my way.

Gunshots followed them, all the way back to me, and the fact that the room was completely trashed slowly seeped into my mind. As in, almost as bad as when we'd first seen it.

Splintering wood and plaster followed my friends, but they weren't shot—neither was I, thank goodness—and they dove behind the door I was hovering near.

"Quick, this way!" I headed back toward the kitchen, but Erik tackled me halfway there and rolled me under the long table, Ari close behind.

She rolled over, and we were face to face.

I snapped my fingers and pointed at her. "Zoë! Zoë Washburne!"

Erik chuckled. "She gets that a lot. *Firefly* fan?"

I nodded and put a hand over my heart. "Best fourteen episodes ever made."

He grinned, a new appreciation on his face. "Don't forget the movie!"

"How could I?" I paled a little. "Except the reaver parts. I couldn't watch those."

Not only was Ari glaring at us like we'd lost our minds, she also looked like she wanted to throttle us both. "Can we please focus here?"

A floorboard squeaked across the room.

Oh, that's right. We were being *shot* at. By a ghost.

Could this night please just be over?

"Wait. Where's —"

Ari clamped a hand over my mouth.

Where are Jer and Harriet? my mind screamed.

Then heavy, dragging footsteps—chains were now somehow involved—came our way and started moving around the table. I squeaked, and the footsteps paused.

Ari elbowed me, murder in her eyes, but after the longest minute in the history of mankind, the footsteps resumed.

And then the table flew to splinters over our heads.

We all started screaming again and scrambling toward the main door—the door farthest away from *her*. Erik and Ari made it around the corner, but the door exploded in my face, and I fell back.

The crazy ghost lady raised her weapon and stared at me. Straight at me, barrel in my face.

Pretty sure I lost ten years off my life right then and there.

"I did it. I killed them. My servants. That whore. My husband. His children. My children." She choked on a sob. "I killed them all! And you're next." An unhinged smile spread across her face. "Dinner is served."

"Y-you don't w-want to do this," I somehow managed. "M-maybe we could t-talk . . ."

And Erik tackled her.

She didn't fall over, which I totally expected for some reason. Her aura just swirled and converged again. Then her image flitted across the room in a jarring motion. Gun still pointed at me.

Erik and I froze.

"Dinner. Is. Served." She pulled the trigger.

Erik pointed behind me and screamed, "Watch out!" as Mrs. Rutherford fired, and I dove for the floor, throwing a frantic look over my shoulder.

The ghost butler was reaching for me, long knife—what

looked like a *real* knife—in hand, cruel sneer on his face, and mid-swing, he dissolved in a spray of red droplets.

The knife clattered to the floor.

I kept screaming. Erik curled up in a ball right there—pretty sure he was screaming too, but I couldn't hear him over my own shrieks—and we paused at exactly the same moment when we realized the rest of the room had fallen eerily silent.

We both turned in slow motion toward the other ghost in the room.

She nodded, satisfied. "Dinner is served." In a blurring motion, she whipped the hunting musket up under her chin and fired.

I screamed. Again. Fortunately for me—because I couldn't look away, not even if my favorite actor, Gavin Bailey, happened to walk by at that very moment—she simply vanished. No spray of blood.

There one moment, gone the next.

We both waited—numb, frozen, emotionally weary and totally spazzed out—for what seemed like an eternity, but she didn't come back.

"Does—does that mean it's over?" My hoarse voice blended with the fading echo of the gunshot.

"Looks like it," Erik said, climbing to his feet. "Come on."

He held out his hand, and I took it, thankfulness filling every pore in my body.

"Hey, thanks for that. You kinda saved my life. I think."

I smiled at him. Although I didn't believe it for a second, Jemma once told me the room lit up when I smile, that it transformed my face into something magnificent.

Completely absurd and not true, but it sure sounded nice.

Dusky red tinged his neck, and he averted his gaze as he hauled me to my feet. "Yeah, um, no problem."

And the room lit up. Quite literally. Quite blindingly, in fact.

Pretty sure that wasn't me.

We both squinted and stared around us, trying to see, but it was so blasted *white*. I couldn't see a thing. The table we'd been hiding under earlier had even disappeared, gunshot holes and everything.

"Guys?" a feminine voice said, muffled and far away.

"Arielle?" Erik answered.

A door slammed, and I may have jumped. I tended to react to e.v.e.r.y.t.h.i.n.g. in everyday life, so just imagine how much worse it was when things got scary.

The blinding light went out, replaced by candlelight, and we were in a completely different room. I mean, completely different.

It was a suave ballroom, smooth wooden floors polished to a high shine, no bullet holes in sight. It was three times bigger than the dining room we were just in, wainscoting carved with unique frescos, a mirror lining one whole wall.

The ceiling was carved with some kind of pattern — square blocks reminiscent of something European — and more frescos were carved into the corner of each high ceiling.

I mean, the place was gorgeous. So freaking gorgeous, I could only spin in a slow circle and stare, mouth wide open.

It was all vibrant, real, no ghostly blue in sight.

What was this place? The absurdity of the situation caught up to me, and I started laughing. And I couldn't stop.

I gasped for breath and held out my hand. "Care to dance?"

Erik batted my hand away. "Be serious." Then he looked wildly about the room. "Ari? Arielle!"

A lead ball dropped in my stomach, and I started to panic. Just a little. Okay, a lot.

"Arielle!" I screeched, adding my hysteria to Erik's.

Deep laughter resonated throughout the room, and Erik and I looked wildly about, trying to find its source. Erik spotted it first and yelped, flinging himself my way.

Of course I would get stuck in here with Shaggy, possibly

the only person on earth more scared than I was. At least he hadn't jumped into my arms, or I would've dropped him. And possibly fallen over myself.

Erik grabbed my arm and pointed. "Um, what's that?"

My eyes riveted on what he was pointing at.

Directly across from us, on the opposite wall as the dining room's organ, an illustrious pipe organ took up the entire wall, climbing through the ceiling in a half-curved area I hadn't noticed. How I hadn't noticed it was beyond me. It was huge!

And it took up one whole wall. Had I mentioned that?

And worst of all, a freaking skeleton sat at the bench, grinning his eternal grin our way, hands poised over the keys.

"Boo," he said.

CHAPTER TWENTY

"Ahh!" we screamed and tried to make our own door in the center of the closest wall.

It didn't even budge. I'd give anything for Scooby-Doo to be real at the moment. Then we could actually make a hole in the wall, and there would be a real, living person behind the mask.

I flicked a glance behind me at the fluidly moving skeleton. Yep, definitely way too much space between those ribs to be a costume.

Please somebody wake me up right now.

I moved to the metal-coated door and pulled and pushed and shoved and didn't give up, no matter how fruitless a part of my brain kept telling me it was. I was getting through that door!

I wiped tears from my eyes and kept pulling. I was crying now? Oh, fantastic.

Deep laughter curled around us and spiraled away. "Oh, come now, don't you like my ballroom?"

I didn't answer, Erik didn't answer—we were intent on getting through that door, metal or no metal.

"Oh, for pity's sake," the skeleton said. "That's enough of that."

Something tugged at my waist and threw me halfway across the room.

Unfortunately, whatever had grabbed me—and it really didn't feel like anything had, just that I'd been hurled for No. Freaking. Reason—had done the same to Erik, and we landed in a tangled heap that hurt a whole heck of a lot.

My parents generally frowned upon cursing, as did my strict Christian school. Had I mentioned that? So substitute words were my go-to in times of stress.

Not important at the moment.

As I groaned and tried to heave Erik's heavy body off me, the deep voice curled around us once more.

"That's better. Did you like my story? Answer truthfully, now."

Erik, now a blubbery mess of snot and tears, pretty much fell off me and couldn't speak, so I started talking. Never a good thing.

"Story? What s-story? W-what do you m-mean?"

He swept his bleached-white hand wide. "Why, my story! The crazed wife and her killing spree!"

My mouth just kind of opened and closed on its own as I made little gasping sounds.

"Well?" He partially stood and made as if to come my way, and I scrambled back. I didn't want him anywhere near me!

"Yes! I mean, no! It was horrible. What do you mean, your story?"

He flipped imaginary coat tails behind him and settled back on the bench, hands hovering over the keys once more. "My masters. Horrible people. They deserved what they got."

He paused, and when I didn't say anything, he turned and looked at me.

"Uh, oh, uh, why did they deserve this?" I stammered.

If a skull could look satisfied, he did as he turned back to his organ. Phantom of the Opera, anyone? Only much, much worse.

I'd take a love-crazed psycho kidnapper-killer over this any day.

Maybe.

"I had to serve those selfish people as they used their wealth, their power, to hurt people. To make others feel small. To ruin reputations and impregnate maids. Someone had to stop it."

I stuttered out, before he could look at me again, "And that someone was you? Why? What did you do? To, uh, stop it." *Just stop talking, Candace. Please.*

His head rotated too far around to look at me as he smiled —well, kept smiling. "Who better to do it than I? I was in the perfect position to drop little hints along the way, drive the madness deeper, plant doubts about the husband in the wife's mind. Plant dissatisfaction deep and root it out when it was time. They never suspected a thing."

I nodded too many times, trying to keep my death as far away as possible. "Uh-huh. Right. Of course. I never suspected a thing either."

Because that made sense.

His voice deepened and rattled the room, hands splayed in the air for his moment of glory. "The master will see you now!"

My jaw fell open. Oh my gosh. It was the freaking butler.

I had to say it. I had to. I nudged Erik. "Hey. Hey, Erik. It was the butler. The butler did it." I snort-giggled.

Nothing from Erik. I eyed him. He was drooling a little and staring vacantly into the middle distance. I sighed. Why did I have to be the one keeping a level head and conversing with a skeleton?

Because the universe had it out for me, that's why.

The trembling rumble of his voice snaked into the walls as it faded, and the skeleton slowly turned and looked at me.

I jumped. "B-but the wife. She's the one who pulled the trigger. Right?"

His hands still drifted above the keys, waiting for what I couldn't imagine, and he laughed. "You could say I handed her the ammunition. Lit the fuse. Gave her the encouragement she needed."

"Uh, well, um, that's nice . . ."

Before I finished speaking, he slammed his hands on the keys and rattled everything within a mile. Then he started playing—quite impressively, I might add. But it was so loud, I clamped my hands over my ears.

It wasn't actually Phantom of the Opera music, but it was pretty darn close.

Apparently it was just the jolt Erik needed as well, and he did the same. The skeleton's deep voice rose above the organ music and pounded into my head. I more felt it than heard it, and my chest ached upon impact.

"Welcome to my freak show!"

Not corny. Not corny at all. It was actually quite terrifying, but I couldn't imagine telling someone about this without sounding like a nut job.

He let the notes fade for a few beats, then he slammed his hands on the organ's keys again. The instrument wailed even louder and elicited a scream from me.

Flames blazed on either side of him and washed us with heat, coming out two open pipes on either side of the organ, and caught the room on fire. Smoke began billowing as the flame crept up the walls and engulfed the gorgeous ceiling and wainscoting.

"No!" Erik snapped upright. "You monster, those frescos are some of the most gorgeous I've ever seen. They're historic masterpieces!"

I tugged on Erik's arm as he strained toward the skeleton, hands outstretched like he was going to strangle it.

"Erik! Erik, can you hear me?" He dragged me a few steps. "You really don't want to do this. Erik!"

He looked back at me, seemed to realize what he was doing, then shook his fist at the skeleton and stopped trying to drag me toward the demonic thing.

A sort of relieved giddiness bubbled up in me, and I snorted a laugh. "So am I gonna say the butler did it or are you?"

Erik scrunched his forehead. "Uh, Candace, not really the time or place."

Like he had any room to talk.

I looked at him, my brain slowly starting to work again. "Escape?"

"Yes. Please. Let's."

We bolted toward the only door in the place—the one leading to the foyer—and the metal sheeting was gone.

I pounded on the heavy wood. "Ari! Ari? Can you hear us?"

"Open the door, Arielle!" Erik called.

Something exploded behind us. We both hunched down, and I turned to look. The organ was in charred fragments.

Something black lifted off the skeleton. The skeleton fell to the floor, lifeless and breaking into a million pieces, and the dark spirit plunged into the floor, tearing up a huge section of the gorgeous dance floor.

I mean, seriously? What was wrong with this vengeful spirit or whatever it was?

It tore out of another spot, creating crater *número dos*, then flung itself toward the ceiling and started doing a few laps in a mad dance of terror.

"What is your problem?" Erik screamed. "Leave the dang floor alone!"

Smoke billowed up the walls, and it barely penetrated my brain that some kind of ventilation was keeping us from dying from smoke inhalation. Should've been my first clue that something weird was going on, but duh. Fire and exploding floorboards!

Just a little busy here.

As it dove through the floorboards and made a third crater, Erik hurled himself at the door, muttering about spirits with no respect. I tried to match my hurling to his, but we never exactly found our stride.

"Come on!" I cried more to myself, venting a little terror and frustration. Which, of course, came back in spades.

He turned the knob, and the door swung open. I tumbled after him, falling through the open doorway, right onto his back. He scrambled out from under me and ran straight for the front door.

My body apparently decided it was giving up and refused to move.

I didn't agree with it. I tried to get up, but my knees buckled and I fell. Seriously?

I lay there, dazed and sore and weary and wondering if these were going to be the last few moments of my life, when I noticed something weird.

Erik didn't stop at the front door, pounding away at it as we'd been doing all night. No, he pulled it open and ran straight out the wide-open door and into the night.

The night. It was still nighttime, but lightening by degrees. Was it—was it—I gasped and tried to breathe but could barely get a lungful of air—was it almost daylight?

I shuddered as another crash sounded behind me.

I crawled my way over to the door and up the five steps that led to outside and freedom. The ballroom continued to be trashed behind me, but I just couldn't make myself turn around and look.

And excuse me if I got some kind of perverse pleasure cackling about my favorite line of the evening. "The butler did it. Of course."

My mind wasn't splintering from stress. Not at all.

Something swooped over my head, and I cringed down on the threshold, curling into a ball of terror-paralyzed goo. Now if I could just be brave enough to fall out the door and tumble down the outside steps.

No such luck.

Just as I was peeking over the threshold, telling myself to go ahead and escape already, myself told me right back, "Wait. The dare."

I dropped my head with a sob. The money. I'd forgotten. I needed that money to graduate.

I kind of wanted to live, though, so oh well. I'd graduate next semester.

I lifted my head with difficulty. Now to get off the floor.

Another crash rooted me to the spot. I brought my hands to my ears as I curled tighter into myself. This was it. I was going to die. And I was too much of a coward to do anything about it. Someone was going to have way too much fun carving out my headstone. *Girl dies of fright, inches from escape.*

Or maybe that would be the newspaper headline.

A great big splash followed by a burbling, sucking noise sounded as part of my brain told me the ballroom was going under the swamp again—the other part didn't care—then the racket faded altogether.

My ears rang with ghostly echoes of all the noise as it was siphoned away by time and silence, and it took me a while to realize new noises weren't presenting themselves.

Was it gone? Was this mad night over? Had everything gone back to normal?

Did I even want to look?

I slowly lifted my head and peeked behind me, and although the dim outside light showed settling dust, everything was still. Silent. Trashed. Not lit up by ghost lights.

The same wreck it had been when we'd first come in here. When I didn't have gray hairs.

Oh my gosh, it was over.

"Whoa, I wasn't expecting you to be the last one," said a very masculine and human-sounding voice.

I shrieked and whirled around, tumbling down the steps and landing on my butt back inside the house. I looked up to find an outstretched hand from someone *alive* and not a ghost reaching down to me from the threshold.

I just stared at it. Then at him.

Tyler stared back with wide eyes, then he burst out laughing. "Did you guys see that? Priceless!"

James already had his trusty camera zoomed in on my face.

Stewart elbowed Tyler aside. "Can't you see she's in shock?" He knelt next to my crumpled form. "Hey, Candace, you okay?" He dusted off several poofs of dirt. "Whoa, girl, you smell like smoke."

I looked up into Stewart's face with a "duh" look. Hadn't he seen the fire on all those cameras of his? Hadn't he *set* the fire?

"What happened?" James asked. "We saw a few things move, but the feeds fritzed out about the last half-hour or so, so we headed over here as fast as we could."

What happened? I couldn't even. "Help me up."

They did.

"Now, get me out of here."

They did.

CHAPTER TWENTY-ONE

They hauled me outside and deposited me on a crumbling stone bench across from the manor. Stewart draped a blanket over my shoulders.

James disappeared for a moment and came back talking to someone behind him. Ari rounded the corner, trailing James, looking sullen.

"Arielle!" Erik ran to her and wrapped her in a hug, his eyes closed.

My eyes filled with tears. I was so glad she was okay.

Tyler was bouncing all over the place, like he couldn't contain his excitement. "Psych!"

I stared, bleary-eyed, at the three goons who were beside themselves with giddiness. They wouldn't look that way if they'd just had the all-nighter I'd had.

"We got you good!"

"All the ghosts . . ."

"All that screaming . . ."

"It was epic."

They were high-fiving themselves all over the place. And I was looking to land some punches.

Stewart must've seen the look on my face, because he

elbowed the other guys, and they toned down their celebration a bit.

"It was all a . . . joke?" I bit off each word.

James chuckled uneasily. "Does it matter? You stayed all night. You got the five grand!"

"And the extra grand," added Tyler, "since you were the last one there and all. Didn't think that was going to happen!"

He laughed, and it was too much.

I stumbled to my feet and took several steps forward, but Stewart and James were there, each catching an arm and hauling me back to the bench.

"Easy there, Candace. Just breathe. In and out. There you go." Stewart patted my arm.

Just breathe? Just breathe? I wanted to become a dragon at that very moment and breathe fire all over *them*. Give *them* the biggest scare of their lives.

I was gonna kill 'em.

My mouth started blathering all over the place. "What about the skeleton playing the organ? How did you pull that one off?"

They all looked at each other.

"Skeleton?" Tyler asked. "Whoa, there, Candace. Sure you didn't hit your head or something?"

My glare cut off his nervous chuckle. I wasn't done. "And all that gunfire? Were you trying to kill us?"

"Gunfire?" James looked incredulous, like he was trying to figure out what I was up to. "There wasn't any gunfire."

I threw my hands out to the sides. "And locking us in? How dare you! What if the whole place had caught on fire, huh? How would we have gotten out?"

"Locked you in? Fire?" James looked like he didn't know how to answer me. "Candace, what are you talking about? You could've left at any time."

I slashed my hand through the air and growled a little. "Really? What about those metal hurricane shutters? Over all the doors and windows. How were we supposed to get through those, huh? How could you?"

I choked under the onslaught of my all-over-the-place emotions and hoped I wasn't about to burst into tears.

Stewart held up his hands in a gesture of peace. "Honest, Candace, we didn't do any of that. See?"

He held out a tablet, pulling up the live feed inside the house and scrolling back to earlier.

"This is what we caught. See? Our fake ghosts? You guys running and screaming? A few special effects? That's all."

Tyler snorted. "Special effects. If you mean firecrackers from the discount store, sure." He glanced at me and held up a hand. "Just to make you guys jump a few times, of course. Nothing dangerous at all."

Stewart gave him a look, one that said, "I'm trying to calm this crazy chick down and you're just making it worse!" Or perhaps more accurately: "You're an idiot."

I'd go with that one.

I went back to staring at the little screen. Unbelievable. The ghosts were gray, not blue, and so digitally fake, I couldn't even.

I looked into Stewart's eyes, so somber and serious, like he wanted me to believe every word he was saying.

"Those aren't even the same ghosts!" I shouted, right in his face.

Erik and Ari crowded me, and after they'd viewed the footage, the three of us blathered over each other, trying to describe everything we'd seen.

"You're telling us you didn't do any of that stuff?" Ari demanded.

All three guys shook their heads.

"Not even," said James. "*We* don't even know that much history about this place. We just wanted something fun for our site. You know, to celebrate the anniversary of the unsolved murder."

Now we were all spooked. Our eyes turned as one toward the plantation from hell.

"Let's, uh, get out of here. Talk about it over pizza at my place?" Stewart offered.

We all tried to run over each other to get back to the cars and leave this wreck of a nightmare behind. The sprint down the weed-infested dirt drive seemed to take years.

No one spoke until we'd gone past the "No Trespassing" signs.

"What about Jer and Harriet?" I asked.

The guys glanced at each other. James answered. "Oh, they're fine. They found one of the ways out and took it. Seriously, you guys could've opened a door or window at any time. You would've been disqualified, sure, but we weren't trying to trap you or anything."

Ari, Erik, and I all looked at each other for a split second before I shouted, "Would that be the door covered by metal sheeting or the window covered by metal sheeting?"

All three guys held up their hands in the universal sign of surrender, and we booked it even faster to the front gate, wrapped firmly shut in a million, bazillion chains.

Maybe that should've been our first warning. After the murder. And the ghost sightings. And the absurd amount of cash. And the "I don't think so" from every other sane person in the world.

Peter, Jer, and Harriet were waiting for us outside the gates we had to climb over.

I was still so shaky, when I reached the top, I fell over the other side and had to lay there for a minute until my whole body stopped screaming in pain.

Once we'd determined nothing was broken—and once the gang got me going again with words like "police" and "cops" and "trespassing" and "jail"—I walked straight up to Harriet and gave her a hug.

"I'm so glad you're not dead."

She peeled me off her and set me far away. "Girl, don't be weird."

Jer and Peter looked like they didn't know what to do with that either.

I sniffled. Even though I hated her guts, I didn't want her to die because of a stupid dare or stupid ghosts. I nodded and wiped my nose with the back of my hand.

I staggered past them to Peter. I tried to hug him, but he held me at arm's length, eyeing my snot-smeared hand. "Ugh. You look awful. And you smell worse."

He pushed me aside and headed straight for the three guys. I could only stare at him with my mouth open.

"So she did it, right? She gets the five grand?" His eyes widened. "No wait. Six grand!"

I thought he was going to break out in an Irish jig right there. And he wasn't even Irish.

I wasn't the only one glaring at him. Our three friends plus Ari looked like they wanted to shut him up in the haunted mansion. For life. Or bury him alive in a casket.

I might have hammered in a few nails myself.

Stewart's jaw ticked. "That's between her and us."

I nodded. *That's right.* No way was I trusting him with any of my money ever again.

Stewart turned and gave me a high-five, grin overly bright to compensate for Peter's stupidity. "Great job, you did it! Told you you could."

I raised my hand out of reflex, nothing else. I was entirely too numb to think clearly.

Peter edged Stewart aside and dropped his arm around my shoulders, touching me as little as he could.

"We should celebrate. Olive Garden? I have so many ideas about that money—"

Oh no he didn't. He wasn't spending my money. Not this time. I shrugged him off and glared.

"It goes on my school bill. All of it. If you want to take me out after I've paid off my bill—and pay for my meal and yours"—something he rarely did—"then we'll talk." I held up my hand when he opened his mouth. *"After* I've paid my bill."

I walked away from him, and Stewart dropped his arm around my shoulders instead, a satisfied look on his face.

"All right. So let's pay off this school bill." He winked. "After pizza."

I beamed at Stewart and didn't even care that Peter was glaring daggers our way.

"So you guys were just joking, right?" Erik asked later, as we stood around our cars outside of Stewart's place, far away from the place I was never, ever going to again, not for twenty million dollars. "About not setting that all up?"

I didn't miss the glance the guys shot each other—they were as spooked as we were—but apparently Peter took Erik's question as a yes.

Peter laughed. "Good one . . ."

He held up both hands to high-five the guys. They all gave him stony looks and walked away.

My anger toward them eased.

If they thought it wasn't cool he'd ditched me in that house, lost my money, and put me in this position in the first place, maybe they weren't all that bad.

As long as they never did anything like this to me again for the rest of my life.

CHAPTER TWENTY-TWO

I stood in line at the school business office, aka the on-campus bank, as a flurry of seniors rushed in and out, paying off last-minute fines, tuition fees, and anything else that would keep them from graduating.

As I waited impatiently, I bounced on the balls of my feet, totally freaking out. I'd never had so much money in my life, and I was terrified the police would pop out of nowhere and cart me off to jail for . . . something illegal. Like breaking and entering.

Demerit magnet, remember? I just bet that went for jail time too.

Finally, after the most excruciating half-hour of my life, I arrived at the little window and stared at the calm teller. Or whatever her position was.

She gave me a plastic smile. "Yes? How may I help you today?"

I slid my student ID her way, and she tapped out my info. Once she'd pulled up my student file, she smiled at me expectantly.

I cast a nervous little glance at the teller next door. The frazzled one. At first I was thankful I hadn't gotten her—over-reaction was her strong suit—but now the calm, "I have every-thing under control" person was freaking me out just as much.

"My, um, my school balance? My bill? My school balance of my bill?"

I clamped my lips shut. Why in the blazes did my words think they could just do whatever they wanted whenever I opened my mouth?

My teller scribbled a string of numbers out on a little piece of paper and slid it my way. I read the numbers and sagged. Still $5,897.53.

Oh my goodness, I'd done it. I was going to graduate.

Maybe. I still had to hand over the check.

I slid sweaty palms into my pocket and then shoved the cashier's check her way.

She flipped it over and had me sign it.

Here it came. It wasn't legit. It couldn't be. She was going to have me arrested.

She didn't bat an eye. Just started depositing. "You do realize the check will need to clear before the balance will be credited to your account, yes?"

I mouthed yes, the words not making it past my squeaky throat. I cleared my throat and tried again. "Yes."

"Good. It should clear tomorrow. Since it's a cashier's check." She stared at me expectantly.

I jumped and slid another check her way. From Peter. For the senior portraits.

I had already signed it "For Deposit Only." No way was I signing my name ever, ever again. Or trusting someone else to deposit them.

I frowned as half of the amount it should've been went into my account, thanks to Peter.

Oh, he'd deposited them, all right. He'd deposited them right into a big, fat down payment on two duplex-style apart-ments, side by side, in Acción. I still saw red every time I thought about it.

Even though he'd sworn up and down he hadn't misunderstood on purpose, forcing me to go to that stupid haunted house *or* Acción, I was having a hard time believing him.

Yeah, right.

But at least he'd given me the half he'd put on his apartment back. That was something, right? And all the flowers and chocolate and apologies . . .

She finished making the deposit and looked my way. "And the remaining balance?"

Oh my gosh, did I owe more than she'd told me?

"Do you want cash back? Or the balance deposited into your bank account?"

It took me a moment to realize that after paying off my school bill, I had money left over.

Oh. Big relief. No jail time. Yet.

Since the school's business office doubled as the bank on campus, I squeaked, "I'd like the rest to go into my personal account. Please."

Again, it didn't even faze her. She typed it all in with the enthusiasm of a robot. "No withdrawals today?"

I blinked. I hadn't even considered that. It had been so long since I'd had spending money of any kind . . . "Um, twenty? No, one hundred!"

Giddiness swamped me. All that cash in one place . . .

She had me sign the withdrawal slip, counted out five beautiful twenties, all crisp and new, and handed me the receipt with a bright smile and a "thank you."

I nodded and stared between the millions of dollars I was holding and the balance there. $502.47. I was rich.

I shoved the cash in my pocket, my mind whirling with ideas. What was I going to do with it? Eat some real food off campus? Pay someone to work one of my shifts so I could take a nap? Just stare at it for a while?

A little dizzy, a lot off-kilter, I ambled out of the office, staring at my balance the whole way.

I was used to lots of zeros, sure, but it was always going to the school, not me.

I had a nice little nest egg to start my life in Acción, New Mexico. I scrunched my nose. Did anyone even say "nest egg" anymore?

"Hey, watcha doing?"

I jumped a mile and spun to face Jackson, my heart in my throat. "Oh! It's you!"

That was me: bright and quick witted. Not sure why Jackson even tried to speak to me in the first place.

His smile was sincere. "Sorry, didn't mean to scare you. Get some good news or something?"

I tilted my head, and he nodded at the scrap of paper in my hand.

"Your smile could light a football field."

"Oh!" I flushed and shoved it deep in my pocket. "You could say that, yeah."

"Great. I'm glad." His smile hinted that he knew what it might be.

He had given me the flyer for the Rutherford Hall dare, after all. And now that all my screaming was live for the world to see, he quite possibly had watched it, but I wasn't thinking about that right now. If ever.

He shoved both hands in his pockets and rocked up on the balls of his feet, then back on his heels. "So, uh, I've been meaning to ask you . . ."

"Candace!"

As if everything turned to slow motion, I careened toward the voice. Yep. Peter, heading my way. Smile as plastic as my teller's and a lot more hostile.

Oh no. *So* not good.

Why, you may ask? Because I was talking to another guy. But not just any other guy, *the* hottest guy on campus. And enough girls talked about Jackson that steam was not literally rolling out of Peter's ears, but it could've been.

Maybe Jemma had a point. Or three.

He came up and slipped an arm around my waist and kissed me, right there, in front of Jackson and passing students and the help desk lady. The strict help desk lady.

She cleared her throat, and Peter looked her way. "Oh, I'm sorry, Mrs. Pruet."

She smiled at him. "It's quite all right, dear. Just maybe not here?"

I blinked, and my jaw may have dropped open. Was this the same lady who'd threatened to have me kicked out of school when my brother had visited and I'd hugged him?

How Peter had every old lady in the school wrapped around his finger, I had no idea. He didn't even have *me* wrapped around his finger.

Something I really needed to think about, according to Jemma. Maybe later?

His smarmy grin was just so . . . smarmy. "Of course, Mrs. Pruet." He turned back to Jackson, and everything went flat — his eyes, his smile, his voice. "What are you doing here, Holmes?"

Jackson kept one hand in his pocket, but the other gripped the strap of his messenger bag. "It's a free country, Smythe."

I squirmed a little. Okay, a lot.

"So it is." Peter turned and steered me away. "And we were just leaving."

I dug in and stayed where I was. "Hold it." I twisted to look Jackson's way. "You had something to ask me?"

He softened a little, started to say something, then looked at Peter, who still had his arm around my waist. I was almost certain Mrs. Pruet was going to shoot us with a laser gun any second.

Hey, watch enough *Star Trek* with your brother and tell me laser guns don't pop into your head every once in a while, either. (I know, I know, technically it's a phaser, but copyright infringement and all . . .)

Jackson shook his head. "You know what? Forget it."

He turned and walked away, shaking his head every few steps.

I had no clue what that even meant, and I wasn't about to try to figure it out. Men.

Peter smirked and tugged me toward the front door. "So," he said, his nonchalance as false as a plastic flower. So many plastic similes when it came to Peter. "What were you and Holmes talking about?"

I stared at him. "Holmes?"

He sighed, deep and impatient. "Jackson."

"Oh."

How had I not known his last name? Because names were only invented to trip me up, that's why.

I shrugged. "I have no idea." I elbowed him, my words light, but I was annoyed to no end. "I totally would've found out had you not interrupted."

"Wouldn't that be just great," he muttered under his breath as if I couldn't hear him. "Bummer," he said louder.

I snorted. "Right."

He rounded on me. "What's that supposed to mean?"

Really? He was going to do this? After he'd apologized all over the place and groveled and said he was losing his mind because he didn't know what would happen to us if I ended up not going to Acción because I couldn't pay my bill and that was the only reason he'd acted so crazy over the whole dare?

But the business office hallway was not the place to have argument *número dos*.

I held up my hands, the universal sign for surrender, my smile falsely bright. Hey, two could play this game. "Oh, nothing. See you tomorrow for lunch!"

And I left him in the dust. I was one of those fast walkers who could weave in and out of crowds without touching anyone, usually faster than anyone could catch up, and it annoyed Peter to no end.

Did everything I do annoy him?

Something to think about. Later.

Although I'd never admit it, I may have done it on purpose this time.

Right now, I had to get to the first of my senior photo shoots. Even if I wasn't getting paid for them. At least, it didn't feel like it anymore. Then take my first final.

Then graduate.

Peter was promptly forgotten as I did a little happy dance and sprinted down the hall.

CHAPTER TWENTY-THREE

I photographed Jemma's wedding, covered in scratches and bandages.

Besides fussing at me for letting Peter talk me into anything, much less going to a freaking haunted mansion for a freaking sleepover, Jemma didn't mind the fact that I looked like a freaking mummy.

Night of the living dead, anyone? No? Good answer.

So I moved around her wedding, trying to remain invisible, be unobtrusive, yet capture those shots that I knew would mean the world to her.

And you know what I hated myself for? Jackson was there —he'd stayed after graduation—and I kept looking for him, then jerking my head away every time I saw him or our eyes met. For some reason. Don't ask me why.

And you know what was even worse? I was so thankful Peter had gone on to Acción without me. He was driving me just a little bit batty. Make that a lot batty.

Had to be the stress of graduation. Had to be.

Bryan and Jemma were pronounced man and wife, kissed each other for way too long, Bryan's fist in the air in a victory punch—best pictures ever—and then turned to their guests, beaming for all the world to see.

I zoomed in on their faces for a few shots, and I just couldn't get over how much Jemma was glowing. I mean, seriously glowing. Her eyes sparkled, and she stared up at Bryan with the most loving, adoring gaze I'd ever seen on a person's face.

My heart squeezed, and I swallowed hard to dislodge the choking feeling from my throat, but the burn remained.

I must've been overtired. Getting scared to death at a real haunted mansion would do that to a person. Plus graduating, preparing for a new job in a new town, my boyfriend going all psycho on me, and then apologizing all over the place . . .

The beat picked up, and Bryan and Jemma and their wedding party started rocking some moves.

Bryan and Jemma danced their way down the aisle to the music, and I rushed to stay ahead of them, my steps morphing into a weird little jig on their own. Hey, the song called for it.

It was perfection. (The wedding, not my dancing.)

They stopped around the corner and started making out—I mean, like, Making. Out.

I started to take a picture, hesitated, then walked away. I'd give them a moment or three.

After they decided to come up for air—which if I were being honest, I wasn't exactly sure was gonna happen—I cautiously approached them, not quite making eye contact.

"So, um, you want posed pics next?"

Jemma cackled—and believe me, her cackle was somehow elegant; I didn't even know how such perfect people existed—and she threw her arm around my shoulders.

"You should see your face, Marshall. Beet, cherry-tomato, fire-engine red."

I couldn't help my grin. "Oh, is that all?"

"Yup."

I went back to business, my safe zone when people tried to draw me into small talk or add to my humiliation.

"So, um, pictures?" I held up my camera.

She danced back over to her husband and hugged him, staring up at him with adoring eyes. "I don't want any stuffy, posed pictures. Just make sure you capture us with family, yes?"

I sniffed, affronted. "Of course."

She came over and dropped a kiss on my cheek, something she'd never done before, and grinned at me a bit drunkenly. Though happy drunk, not drunk drunk, since her family didn't drink, either.

I'm telling you, strict Christian schools were the places to find these kinds of people, and they actually existed. Really. It was kind of nice not to have to explain myself every time I turned down a drink.

"Like I need to tell you how to do your job. Just work your magic, and I will be perfectly happy!"

I grinned. She already was.

She latched back on to her husband, unable to be away from him for more than a few seconds, and they made their way to the open white tent on the beach. In the church's backyard. Talk about prime real estate.

I slipped off my rhinestone-encrusted sandals and followed.

The setting sun was the perfect background, and I got some gorgeous shots—and lots of kissing pictures. I'm telling you, so many.

I'd upped my nighttime shooting game since finding out the wedding would be so late. Thank goodness for all the bonfires prepped and ready to go. Now to perfectly execute everything I'd learned and practiced.

But the sun would shine for another hour or so, so I would take advantage of the light while I could. I got just a little sweaty thinking about messing up any of Jemma's pictures.

But I needn't have worried. Jemma had prayed everything

would go just as God wanted it to, and man, her prayers worked. It was a dream wedding. I had, like, maybe three bad shots. Out of a thousand.

I get a little trigger happy when I have a camera in my hands, okay?

The dancing started, and I got father-daughter shots, mother-son shots, and lots and lots of fun shots.

Then I melted into the background, on the prowl for those one-of-a-kind snapshots that only came by accident. Plus I was dying of thirst.

Erik and Ari drifted by.

"Hey, Marshall." Ari gave me a fist bump.

I juggled my camera and the drink I'd almost gotten a sip of and managed not to drop either while returning said fist bump. Mad skills right there. Plus, camera strap.

Still, it was me, and I didn't want to mess anything up.

"Candace!" Erik gave me a warm hug, and my face flamed to ten times its normal hue. He finally pulled away after a million years, and I fanned myself and pretended not to notice I'd made a fool of myself yet again.

Hey, I wasn't used to open affection, okay?

His hands rested on my shoulders. "Good to see you!"

I stammered something in response, then he wrapped his arm around Ari's shoulders. Ari gave me a mild look, hopefully not too offended that a simple, friendly hug could reduce me to an embarrassed mess.

"Got plans after graduation?" Ari asked.

I nodded too many times, gulped down my drink, and licked my lips. "Yes, um, I'm moving to Acción. New Mexico. To be a copy editor. At a newspaper."

"Nice!" Now Erik gave me a fist bump.

I gave him a shy smile. I wasn't so sure about that, but I'd take it.

"You dump that pathetic excuse for a boyfriend yet?" Ari asked point blank.

My mouth fell open.

Erik looked uncomfortable for the first time ever. "Ari." He nudged her and gave me an apologetic look. "She didn't mean it."

"I did mean it. I'm just saying what we're all thinking." Her eyes rested on me, not letting me out of this one.

I mumbled and stammered some more, something about "he apologized" and "he said he was sorry, like, a bunch" and "flowers" and "I think he feels really bad" and a few other things that sounded stupid even to me.

"Uh-huh," Ari said.

Erik used his lanky build to wind himself around Ari and steer her toward the dance floor. "We're, uh, just gonna go now . . ."

"See you around, Marshall. Best of luck," Ari said and let herself be steered.

"Yeah, keep in touch!" Erik added as he walked backward a few steps.

Ari gave me a ghost of a smile that was gone before I could even be sure it was there, then their focus was on each other.

I let out a huge breath, heaved my empty cup into the nearest trash can, and followed at a distance, ready to get back to pictures and non-small-talk situations. Especially those of the uber-uncomfortable persuasion.

My comfort zone lasted, like, three seconds.

Don't ask me how, but I knew Jackson was standing next to me before he'd even cleared his throat.

"So, um, want to dance?"

I wielded my camera like a weapon. "Can't. Taking pictures. Sorry."

I pretty much said it before he'd gotten all the words out of his mouth. Don't ask me how, but I knew he was going to ask. And I really, really wanted to say yes.

Was that bad, since I was dating someone else?

Jemma glided by and snatched the camera out of my hand,

gracefully unlooping its strap from around my neck at the same time. She blew me a kiss. "Sure you can. I'll just take this off your hands for a sec."

And the bride starting snapping pics of her guests. Strap firmly around her neck. She knew how I felt about my camera.

Uncanny timing, that one.

Jackson smiled. "So I guess you're free."

My shy smile matched his. "So I guess I am."

As he slid his hand around my waist, I had trouble breathing. I glanced around, certain I shouldn't be doing this, and sure enough, Miss Redhead from before, from the school hallway, was glaring in my direction.

At least dorm-room girl wasn't here. She might've launched herself at me right then and there.

Thinking about her and her heartbreak if she could see me now brought on even more guilt. I hated offending people. Any people. Even people I didn't know.

Jackson tugged me gently to the dance floor.

I stumbled after him. "Um, well, maybe this isn't such a good idea."

I might break something. Including but not limited to: my heart, his ankle, and any furniture or decorations nearby.

His smile was just the slightest bit intoxicating. And I knew for a fact it was his smile, because there was no champagne at this wedding.

His tone was gentle. "I think it is."

My dancing was totally wooden in his arms—I loved to dance, so this was just embarrassing—and we didn't say much.

I cleared my throat. "So, um, you had something to tell me. Earlier. Before we were interrupted. Outside the school business office?"

It looked as though he found the memory just about as pleasant as I did. His frown was fleeting, though. "I hear you're moving to Acción with Peter."

I flushed deep red. "Well, not *with* him. We have our own places and everything." *Thank goodness.*

"But you're still dating him, right?"

Why did everyone want to know this all of a sudden? I sent a suspicious glance Jemma's way. She wouldn't.

And Jackson was still waiting patiently for my answer.

"Oh, um. I think so."

I *think* so? How lame could I get?

He smiled, ducked his head, and drew me just a little closer. I have no clue how, but that open-air tent with cool beach breezes swirling through got stifling. I needed air.

Another breeze swept by. It did, like, no good. None.

He took a deep breath, held it, then said in a rush, "I heard about this intern position in New York City. I know how much you like photography, and as soon as I saw it, I thought it'd be perfect for you."

I gasped, lips parted in surprise. His gaze dipped to my lips. He leaned forward slightly, still staring at them. Then he blinked, shook his head, and twirled me out then back to him.

I swear he maneuvered me just a little bit closer. I fanned myself with one hand. Oh my. What were we talking about again?

"So, anyway, if you're interested, I can send you the info." He shrugged. "If you want."

Interested? Oh, I was definitely interested. Then his words caught up with my brain. Oh! The position. Not him. I knew that.

I shook my head. "I already have a job."

He studied me closely. "Yeah, but is it what you want? Or are you following Peter's dream?"

I tried to protest, I really did, but my words got all tangled up and I just ended up spluttering. A lot.

"Hey, it's okay. You don't have to explain yourself to me. Just think about it. And, well, give me your email so I can send it to you." He gave me a reckless grin.

Half of my face smiled before I could squash it. "I can't. I'm moving to Acción. I already have an apartment, job, plane ticket, everything."

I didn't just up and change my mind and make decisions for myself and things.

He twirled me again, flinging my thoughts away with the motion and slamming the gate on them for good when he pulled me close.

"I just want your email," he whispered in my ear.

"Candy Apple 8,000 at yahoo dot com." It all came out in a rush.

I know, right? Worst email ever.

"See? That wasn't so hard."

His grin was doing weird things to my stomach. Or maybe I'd eaten something I shouldn't have. My eyes widened. That was it! I hadn't eaten yet. That's all it was.

"I wouldn't even know anyone in New York." My protest was beyond feeble.

He shrugged. "You'd know me."

My eyes widened, and there must've been horror all over my face.

He backtracked. Big time. "Or not. It's a big city. We wouldn't even have to see each other. If you didn't want to."

I groaned. That wasn't the problem. He didn't know what he was asking me. "Jackson . . ."

"Actually, my close friends call me Jack. You can too." He smiled. Again. Was he doing that to me on purpose? "And I do know what I'm asking. I'm asking you to find your dream and follow that. No matter the cost."

Huh. Apparently I'd said that out loud. And I didn't know how to respond.

The song came to an end, and I thanked God, my lucky stars, and the Dali Lama that it was finally over.

Jackson held me close for a beat longer, then let me go. "Just think about it."

He kissed my cheek and walked away.

I stared after him like a dummy. A sad, moping, lovesick dummy. *What if?* echoed in my mind, and I squashed it like a bug. I had a plane ticket. A job. A *boyfriend*.

No way could a guy like Jackson be interested in me for more than ten seconds.

Going after my dreams—or another guy, one who might actually treat me with respect—just wasn't possible.

I didn't see Jackson—Jack—again that night.

CHAPTER TWENTY-FOUR

I edited the final photograph and sat back, the blissful faces of Bryan and Jemma Cartwright staring back at me.

I'd never seen a better-looking couple.

Seriously.

Jemma was gorgeous, but she didn't care. She'd always just been friends with everyone, no matter how many guys had asked her out, until she'd met handsome, nearly perfect Bryan Cartwright. I had to admit, he was handsome in the model, movie-star kind of way.

Jemma deserved it—she totally did—but part of me had a hard time wrapping my head around Jemma snagging someone so dashing. She hadn't settled.

And there had been so many guys who'd wanted to date her.

But she'd known, just *known*, exactly who she'd been holding out for when she met him.

I'd snagged the first guy who'd shown a smidgeon of interest, and I couldn't say I was entirely happy. But I was also too scared to see if anyone else was interested. I mostly ran when above-average, good-looking guys tried to have a normal conversation with me.

Take Jackson, for instance. Jack. Whatever.

Why'd he have to up and change his name on me now? I had enough trouble with my own name. Though he'd implied we were now friends. Close friends . . .

"Ugh." I groaned and buried my face in the couch cushion next to me.

After our disastrous conversation at Jemma's wedding, where I'd barely said two words to him—and those were stupid—I hadn't been brave enough to open the email he'd sent me.

I'd hid it, unopened, in one of my folders. Not that Peter snooped, but just in case.

I'd look at it later. Maybe. If bravery and realizing hopes and dreams suddenly became a thing for me.

But I couldn't get Jackson's words out of my head.

Could I do that? Be brave enough to go after my dreams instead of walking the path laid out for me?

That just wasn't me. I was a pushover. I let people make plans for me.

Which is the only reason on planet earth I'd move to the desert. I hated the desert. It was so dry and hot and desert-y there. The ocean was my happy place.

After we'd danced, I hadn't seen Jackson for the rest of the reception. I'd hid behind my camera and pretended it didn't bother me, but oh, it had. Tons.

I let out another groan.

Normal was so not my thing. Unfortunately. I was as awkward as they came. Or so Peter had pointed out at every possible moment with his teasing and not-so-subtle jabs.

I checked the clock on my laptop's screen. Four hours till my flight.

I quickly dropped Jemma's edited files into our shared online folder, then tapped out a text.

If you can stop sucking face for two seconds, you might want to check your Dropbox.

And I hit send.

I stared at my screen in horror. Why did my brother's beyond-horrible description of kissing have to surface now? I smacked my forehead.

"Seriously, Candace? Seriously?" I whisper-shrieked. I chewed on my fingers and waited for her reply, holding my breath. Praying it had somehow gotten lost in the ether.

Her reply came after the most agonizing seconds in my life. *Good one, Marshall.*

I deflated like a balloon. Oh well. Guess I was going with it.

I love you, too. And you're welcome.

I got a smiley face back. Then silence.

Good thing. I didn't even want to know what my sleep-deprived brain would think of next.

I gathered my luggage and popped my head into the next room. "I'm ready to go to the airport."

One of the groomsmen—Dean, was it?—tore his eyes away from his video game long enough to glance at the room's clock. "You sure? It's pretty early."

I hedged. I didn't know the guy, and I definitely didn't want to offend him.

"Um, yes? Please? Maybe? I can wait until you're done with this level, though. No problem. I don't mind."

Actually, I did mind, but I wasn't going to tell him that. Now that I had nothing urgent to distract me, I just wanted it over with.

He grunted and swiftly defeated Jemma's little brother. Her house, her entire family, everything belonging to Jemma, was gorgeous, just like her. Including her friends.

Dean flashed a far-too-white, far-too-handsome smile in my direction. "I'll just get my keys."

He missed my answering smile because it was too slow making its way to my face. What was it with hot people derailing the intelligence I was sure was in there somewhere?

He couldn't get me to the airport fast enough.

Even though Dean wanted to chat, was uber-polite, and took the scenic route, I gave short answers and hurried his easily meandering car along in my mind. Even if it was a classic car he was rightly proud of and I was curious about.

Still, I didn't know enough about cars to have a real conversation about them anyway, so I just didn't.

Also, I didn't want to give Peter any cause to be jealous. If he ever found out who'd taken me to the airport, that is. Or who had danced with me at the wedding.

Ugh. My life, right?

I thanked Dean, waving off his help, then wheeled my luggage to the window, thankful when the officer told him to move his car.

In a flurry, I checked everything in, made my way through security, then sat at my mostly empty gate, not even able to read the first line of the book I'd brought with me.

I let out a deep sigh and stared out the wall of windows at the arriving and departing planes. In a few hours, my flight would arrive and take me to a whole new beginning. A beginning I wasn't even sure I wanted. I sighed again.

I guess I was going to Acción.

CHAPTER TWENTY-FIVE

"That's the girl you hired?"

The man in a sharp business suit smiled, signed something, and handed the clipboard back to his assistant. "That's her."

Tanner's mouth hung open. "Really?"

The man chuckled. "She's perfect."

Tanner looked between the monitor and his boss. "That's what you call perfect? How do you even know she'll do what you want her to do when she gets here? What if she backs out? Or worse, can't perform under pressure?"

The man took a step closer to the monitor, his smile triumphant. "Oh, I know Candace Marshall. Intimately. And one thing I'm certain of: She never backs down from a challenge. She doesn't know it yet, but she's all in."

Tanner shook his head. Ran his fingers through his hair. "If you say so."

"I do."

Tanner shrugged and left without another word.

The man's smile grew as he studied the screen. It was a close-up of Candace, glancing over her shoulder with a worried look, boarding a plane.

Oh, yes. She was perfect.

And soon she'd be in Acción, right where he wanted her.

THE END

Discover Candace's next misadventure in:

ZOMBIE TAKEOVER

Book One of the Candace Marshall Chronicles.

Available Now from L2L2 Publishing.

ACKNOWLEDGMENTS

As with every book of mine, so many people helped make this story what it is.

To my critique group, Mighty Scribblers of the Platform: This book is So. Much. Better because of you!

Cam: Thank you for starting this group! I cannot tell you how helpful it has been. I adore your attention to detail, your encouraging comments, especially when Candace made you laugh aloud, and for putting so much of yourself into your feedback. I treasure every single one of your notes!

Alicia: Girl, I love how you look at a story! You're so objective, no-nonsense, and spot on with your observations and questions. Thank you for making me dig deeper for motivation and propel my characters into greater conflict. You're the best!

Savannah: You're so encouraging! From one editor to another: Thank you for loving how clean my early drafts are! Every time you say that, I die a little from happiness inside. Thank you for making sure this story stayed consistent, and thank you for fangirling with me over the Oxford comma and other grammatical nuances. I'm so very glad Rick Barry introduced us all those years ago!

To my beta readers: TJ, Kara, Lara, Sara, Nicole, and

Cam. Thank you for catching mistakes, letting me know what needed tweaking, and most of all, telling me what you loved! It always makes an author giddy to have their work read in one sitting and then gushed over immediately after. (You know who you are.) Thank you from the bottom of my heart!

To my Snack Pack girls: Alicia, Annie, Kristin, Mackenzie, Rachelle, Savannah. You keep me sane. (Although I am fully convinced we are all insane—in the best way possible!) Thank you for movie nights, Shark Week, endless laughter until our stomachs hurt and certain unnamed individuals roll on the floor and grind leaves into white carpet, plus serious talks and encouragement and text threads. Keep writing!

To my Dream Big Writers Group: Thank you for being a safe haven for me to create these storyworlds! I didn't even know how desperately I needed to stop working to come *write*.

Laura A. Grace, you are just so encouraging! Thank you for your sweet messages, for fangirling over my releases and covers, and for your encouraging book that I read whenever I wonder why I'm doing all this. You make the journey so much lighter! I love you, sweet friend.

Laura VAB and Alena, thank you so much for taking and posting so many pictures of Egypt and Petra when I was unable to go with you! It meant the world. Much of my desperation of not being able to go came out in this book (it pushed me to finish), so although I wasn't able to research the last book in this series (set in Egypt), you helped me finish this book. Thank you for that! And I look forward to asking you a million and one questions about Egypt!

Also, thank you both for fun nights of planning, brain-storming, writing, shooting or sketching cover drafts for our designers, road trips to writing events, and everything else writing and fun related. You are good people!

I also want to thank John Walker and Linda Samaritoni for taking over leadership of the Heartland Christian Writers for me. If not for you both giving me some time back when I was getting overwhelmed, I wouldn't be writing my own stories again. I am so grateful for you both.

To this year's ACFW Indiana board: Linda, Jenny, Rebecca, and Beth. Thank you for the wonderful years serving on the board with you! I have loved it, and I am so grateful to focus on my own writing once again.

To everyone who sent me numerous notes, messages, texts, and emails asking for more of Candace Marshall: This book would not have been born without you. I was thrilled to hear how much you loved my girl. So many hugs!

To everyone who shared my cover, about this release, or absolutely anything else about this book: I am so grateful for you. Thank you for spreading the word!

To Jessica "Faestock" Truscott: Thank you again for the use of your lovely image! You are just the sweetest.

Sara, this cover is glorious! Thank you for taking my idea and making it a thousand times better. I love that ghost so much I can hardly stand it, and I can't get over how you made the text glow. Thank you, thank you, thank you!

To my family: Ben, Blaze, Maverick, Gwenivere, and my mom. I love you all. Thank you for being patient with me, leaving me to my muses, and for being excited when I finished yet another story. Now to get them all published so you can see what I was working on!

And to my readers: I am so thankful for each one of you. Thank you for reading this story, for encouraging me, for asking for more, and for being the best readers an author can have. Here's to many more books to come!

And last but certainly not least, thank you to the Creator of words, who wrote the most timeless and important story ever told. Thank you for sending your Son to die for me, and thank you for creating these worlds with me. All the glory I give to you, and all the mistakes I take for myself. I love you.

In Him,

Michele Israel Harper

ABOUT THE AUTHOR

Michele Israel Harper spends her days as an acquisitions editor for L2L2 Publishing and her nights spinning her own tales. Sleep? Sometimes . . .

She has her Bachelor of Arts in history, is slightly obsessed with all things French—including Jeanne d'Arc and *La Belle et la Bête*—and loves curling up with a good book more than just about anything else.

Author of *Wisdom & Folly: Sisters*, *Ghostly Vendetta*, *Zombie Takeover*, *Beast Hunter*, *Kill the Beast*, and the soon-to-be-released *Silence the Siren*, *Vampire Feud*, and *Queen of the Moon*, Michele prays her involvement in writing, editing, and publishing will touch many lives in the years to come.

Visit www.MicheleIsraelHarper.com or www.L2L2Publishing.com if you want to know more about her!

ABOUT THE AUTHOR

Michele loves to hear from her readers! Follow her on social media, check out her website, or drop her a line to let her know what you thought of Ghostly Vendetta. *Happy reading!*

www.MicheleIsraelHarper.com
Facebook: @MicheleIsraelHarper
Twitter: @MicheleIHarper
Instagram: @Michele_Israel_Harper

REVIEWS

Did you know reviews skyrocket a book's career? Instead of fizzling into nothing, a book will be suggested by Amazon, shared by Goodreads, or showcased by Barnes & Noble. Plus, authors treasure reviews! (And read them over and over and over . . .)

Whether you enjoyed this book or not, would you consider leaving a review on:

- Amazon
- Barnes & Noble
- Goodreads

. . . or perhaps even your personal blog or website or fave social media account? Thank you so much!

—The L2L2 Publishing Team

More from L2L2 Publishing

If you enjoyed this book, you may also enjoy:

Ro remembers the castle before. Before the gates closed. Before silence overtook the kingdom. Before the castle disappeared. Now it shimmers to life one night a year, seen by her alone. Once a lady, now a huntress, Ro does what it takes to survive, just like the rest of the kingdom plunged into despair never before known. But a beast has overtaken the castle; a beast that killed the prince and holds the castle and kingdom captive in his cruel power. A beast Ro has been hired to kill. Thankful the mystery of the prince's disappearance has been solved, furious the magical creature has killed her hero, Ro eagerly accepts the job to end him. But things are not as they seem. Trapped in the castle, a prisoner alongside the beast, Ro wonders what she should fear most: the beast, the magic that holds them both captive, or the one who hired her to kill the beast.

More from L2L2 Publishing

If you enjoyed this book, you may also enjoy:

Huntress Ro LeFèvre is offered a job to hunt a pest plaguing the Seven Seas. A siren has been sinking the king of Angleterre's ships, and in turn, vast amounts of his wealth. Fleeing heartbreak, Ro gladly accepts, but there's just one problem. The king will credit the Marquis de la Valère, and no other women are allowed on the voyage. Ro will just see about that. Hiring an all-female crew without the king's knowledge, Ro hopes they will follow her to the Caribbean, not take the gold and flee. But when Ro is plunged deep into the ocean by the siren she's being paid to kill, presented the sirens' side of the story at knife point, and pressed to join them or die, Ro must decide whether to complete her mission, join the sirens, or something in between. Before the sirens sink her ship.

WHERE WILL WE TAKE YOU NEXT?

Devour *Zombie Takeover*,
Feast on *Beast Hunter*,
Discover *Kill the Beast*,
Relish *Silence the Siren*,
and Soar with *Wisdom & Folly*.

All at
www.love2readlove2writepublishing.com/bookstore
or your local or online retailer.

Happy Reading!
~The L2L2 Publishing Team

ABOUT L2L2 PUBLISHING

Love2ReadLove2Write Publishing, LLC is a small traditional press, dedicated to clean or Christian speculative fiction.

Speculative genres include but are not limited to: Fantasy, Science Fiction, Fairy Tales, Magical Realism, Time Travel, Spiritual Warfare, Alternate History, Chillers (such as vampires, zombies, werewolves, or light horror), Superhero Fiction, Steampunk, Supernatural, Paranormal, etc., or a mixture of any of the previous.

We seek stunning tales masterfully told, and we strive to create an exquisite publishing experience for our authors and to produce quality fiction for our readers.

Ghostly Vendetta is at the heart of what we publish: a fun tale with speculative elements that will thrill our readers.

All of our titles can be found or requested at your favorite online book retailer, local bookstore, or favorite local library.

Visit www.L2L2Publishing.com to view our submissions guidelines, find our other titles, or learn more about us.

Happy Reading!

~The L2L2 Publishing Team